SOUTHERN POTIONS

SWEET TEA WITCH MYSTERIES BOOK NINE

AMY BOYLES

LADYBUGBOOKS LLC

ONE

*I*t was the day after Christmas. The day after the wishing tree had told me my wish was granted, the day after Ellis Mobley had tried to kill me and the day after my cousins' fathers had appeared out of thin air and met them.

Y'all, it had not been a good night.

Mainly because Amelia and Cordelia did not agree on whether their fathers' arrival into town had been a good idea or a bad one.

I was pretty much in there with them.

"Pepper, how's your potion-making kit treating you?"

The four of us—me, Amelia, Cordelia and my grandmother, Betty—sat at breakfast. A bowl heaping with pineapples, grapes and apples squatted in front of me, but I stared longingly at Betty's biscuits and gravy. All the eating I'd done over the holidays presented in my body as a bloated stomach, bloated face and tightened zipper flies. Those sneaky pounds had apparently attached themselves to me, hence the fruit salad breakfast.

I stabbed a pineapple. "The potion kit is going okay. I only just opened it yesterday. Not sure if I'm going to be ready to enter this contest y'all have in Magnolia Cove."

Amelia's eyes flared. "Of course you'll join. Everyone does. Well, everyone who can make a decent potion. That's all of us, of course. Plus the whole town attends the finals." Her gaze drifted to Cordelia. "I'm sure our dads will be there."

Cordelia's hands fisted. Her voice tightened like a guitar string ready to snap. "I don't care if our dads will be there."

"You should," Amelia said smartly. "They're our dads."

Fumes nearly plumed from Cordelia's ears. "Amelia, when are you going to get it in your head that they didn't want anything to do with us? Not one thing. If they'd wanted to be with us, they would've stuck around. They would've stayed. But they didn't. *They left.*"

"They wanted to be here," Amelia argued, "but our moms wouldn't let them."

Cordelia looked like she wanted to launch herself across the table. "Why are you listening to our moms? They're chaos witches. They're barely responsible human beings."

"They're sort of responsible," Amelia whimpered. "Sort of."

Cordelia stabbed her fork into the table. "I'm not going to argue this with you. You can have all the contact you want with your dad and uncle, but I'm not interested. They've had over twenty years to be a part of our lives. Why wait until now?"

"Maybe you had to wish for them." All eyes turned to me. And let me just say they weren't necessarily friendly eyes. I hitched a shoulder. "What? I'm just saying maybe you had to wish for them. With. The. Hat."

I added that because here's the deal—my cousins' fathers are half genie, as in grant-your-wishes genies. Isn't that cool? I thought it was, but the reason why Mint and Licky, my witch aunts, were no longer with the men was because the wishing abilities had gone haywire when Amelia and Cordelia were little.

Things had gotten so bad that Mint and Licky had left their husbands and wouldn't let the men near their daughters in case more bad wishing stuff happened.

As it was, so far Amelia and Cordelia couldn't grant wishes. At least not yet. That was probably for the best.

Amelia twirled her fingers, and food shuffled around her plate. "At some point, *Cord*, you're going to want to know your dad."

Cordelia shrugged. "Maybe. Maybe not. Either way I'll survive, *Am*." Cordelia imitated the way Amelia had shortened her name. Amelia glared at her, and Cordelia smiled. "After all, I've lived this long without knowing them."

"Well it doesn't matter to me," Amelia said. "I'm still going to know my dad."

"Be careful," Betty said.

All gazes flicked to my grandmother, who sat quietly eating biscuits and gravy. There must be an age where you no longer care about what you eat. When one square of chocolate doesn't make you worry that your hips will explode, like it does to me now.

Boy, would I really like to hit that age. Okay, maybe not that age but that attitude.

Yes, I will take the attitude.

Amelia's voice rose in angst. "Why would you say that? Tell me to be careful around my father? It's not like he's an ax murderer."

Betty's mouth twisted into a frown. "I'm only telling you to be careful. Just be careful. Don't think about it too much. Just do it."

Amelia glared at Betty. "You mean something by that."

"I don't mean anything."

"I refuse to believe that." Quiet settled over the room. Amelia didn't let it permeate too long. "Anyway, have y'all heard? It looks like the great potion master Saltz Swift is coming to judge the contest."

"Wonderful," Cordelia said.

"Let me roll out the red carpet," Betty added.

Did I sense a tinge of dislike? "What is it? What's wrong with Saltz Swift?"

"Only that he thinks he's God's gift to potion making," Cordelia said.

"He *is* a potion master," Amelia argued.

"Which would be fine except he walks around wearing flowing white shirts and black leather pants." Cordelia dropped her fork and swiped a napkin across her lips. "If his hair wasn't short and slicked back, I'd swear he was the lead singer in an eighties hair band."

"Well anyway, Saltz is coming. And you know who else is?" Amelia said.

"Who?" Cordelia said, bored.

"Shelly Seay."

Betty's knife clattered to her plate. "Shelly Seay is coming here? To town? I haven't seen her since she lost her job at the school."

I frowned. "What school?"

My question went ignored.

Amelia smiled, obviously proud that she had one-upped Betty on her knowledge. "I heard it from the post office. She sent all her belongings ahead by witch mail. Didn't even bother to bring them with her."

Betty jumped from the table and ran to the door. She shut the blinds and locked all the doors.

I bolted from my chair. Why were we were suddenly in a state of panic? "What's wrong with Shelly Seay? Is she going to destroy the town? Spell us all? What is it?"

Cordelia rushed to the kitchen. She returned and started clearing plates. "Shelly Seay is a sorceress."

"It's only rumored," Amelia said.

Cordelia rolled her eyes. Clearly this was more than rumor. "Right. Okay. Well, it's *rumored* that Shelly is a sorceress. She doesn't always attend the potion-making contest, but when she does, it's believed she pokes around town, asking folks what they're doing. Then she steals the best potion from its maker, tweaks it and wins the contest for herself. If you want to have a fighting chance, the best thing to do is avoid her. At all costs."

I watched as Betty lifted her shotgun, placed her back against the wall and peeked out the blinds.

I shook my head. "I take it that's why we're acting like we're not here. So that Shelly the Sorceress doesn't appear out of nowhere and steal whatever ideas we're working on. By the way, y'all, I have no idea what I'm doing for a potion."

Amelia's face split into a wide smile. "Last year Cordelia made one that bestowed a person with the ability to make smart, sarcastic remarks for exactly thirty minutes."

Amelia clapped with glee. "And I made one that allowed the user to be able to talk to the most boring person ever. I mean, if you were at a New Year's Eve party and got stuck with a dud, this was the potion for you."

I laughed. "Those are hilarious."

"That's the point," Betty said. "It's complete nonsense fun to start the year off with a bang. Most folks in the regular world take this day so seriously—go to the gym, lose fifty pounds. Not us. We have fun."

"But not Shelly," Cordelia said. "She takes it seriously. It's best not to run any risks when it comes to her. Make silly potions—nothing she's going to steal."

"But I don't understand. If she steals the potion, why doesn't the person it was taken from say anything? Accuse her."

Cordelia hitched her brows. "Because they forget."

"Sorcery," Amelia said in a spooky voice.

I rolled my eyes. "Okay. Whatever. I don't even know what potion I'm making, so I doubt she'd be interested in me."

But that was a lie. I totally had an idea for a potion; it's just, until I knew how to make it, I wasn't going to be spouting off about it. You know, there was no reason for people to get excited, especially if I failed miserably.

But maybe the grand potion maker, this Saltz guy, could help me. Since he was a grand potion guy, he had to know something about potions.

"Anyway, the best thing to do is avoid the sorceress." Betty took her place in the rocker, shotgun strapped across her knees. "There's no reason to keep her out of town, but she's no good. There's no doubt about that."

Three hard raps sounded from the door.

"Who is it?" Betty shouted.

"Shelly Seay," came the reply.

My cousins gasped. Now Amelia, I can totally see her freaking out, but to watch Cordelia have that scared response made me nervous. She never overreacted. Which meant Shelly Seay must be pretty freaking awful.

"Hide," Amelia shouted.

"I know you're in there," Shelly said from the other side of the door. "I need to speak to the Craple women."

"We're busy," Betty said.

"I insist," Shelly said. "As a witch I insist you open the door and speak with me."

"You can't just do that," Amelia said. She whipped her head at Betty. "She can't just do that, can she?"

Betty nodded curtly. "She can. Shelly can invoke witch courtesy and demand we speak to her." She lowered her voice. "But only if she invokes it."

Shelly pounded. "I invoke witch courtesy that you open this door right now."

The three of us exchanged a frightened look. "Well," I said, "seems there's no other choice."

TWO

A few minutes later we were having tea with Shelly Seay. She was tall, almost six feet, and wore patterned clothing that reminded me of a reptile. Bright red lipstick glimmered on her lips.

"She probably killed the crocodile herself," Amelia whispered in my ear.

Shelly's dark eyes flashed to my cousin, who quickly zipped her mouth. The sorceress's flowing dark crimson hair hung to her waist. She had high cheekbones, sharp eyes and fashion that looked made-to-order.

She was fabulous, even if she was a sorceress.

"So, how are the Craple women?" Shelly purred.

"Great," Betty said tentatively. "To what do we owe this honor of having you at tea?"

Shelly smiled. It wasn't kind, but it also wasn't unkind. A sort of smile that made you think someone had an extra card up their sleeve —an ace that would transform a situation on a dime.

"You know I always arrive this time of year in preparation for the potion contest."

Betty shoved her corncob pipe in her mouth. "Well you do have to see who you're going to steal from."

Whoa. Betty had no fear.

Not me. I had mountains of fear. You should've seen Shelly—tall and foreboding. There was definitely something powerful if not sinister about her.

But Shelly smirked at Betty's comment. "Funny. No. I'm not here to steal anything. I have a winning potion. One that will knock the socks off Magnolia Cove."

Betty hitched a brow. "What're you telling us for? Aren't you afraid we'll steal it?"

"No, quite the opposite. I need a volunteer to prove what I've done."

"And what is that?" Betty said.

Shelly opened her purse and pulled out a glass-domed cheese plate. That probably wasn't the official name for it. I'm sure it had some sort of witchcraft title that I was naive to.

Anyway, inside sat a green toad. Its throat swelled as if it were about to croak.

"What's that?" Amelia said.

"Not *what*, who?" Shelly countered.

Betty rose. "What sort of black magic is this? We both know you can't change a person into an animal without using the dark arts." She pointed toward the door. "Leave. I don't want the blood of innocents on my hands. Or in my home."

Shelly threw back her head and cackled. "The old always think something dark must be going on."

"*Think?*" Betty snapped. "How about, I know?"

Shelly shook her finger. "You're wrong. That's the old way of crafting, Betty. That's why for years we witches have stayed in the dark, focusing on the ancient methods, the old teachings. I'm trying to create something new. To bring witchcraft into the new millennia."

Betty pressed her finger onto the table. "This is dark magic—blood magic. There's no taking this into the next millennia. What you've called upon by creating this abomination is evil."

Shelly's lips coiled into a serpentine smile. "And what if I told you it wasn't? What if I told you that this was simple potion making." She fingered a tendril of hair from her eyes. "Well, maybe not so simple. But this was done with a potion, not by summoning demons or using blood magic. None of that."

Betty's lower lip trembled. "I don't believe you."

Shelly's eyes flared with glee. "What if I could prove it?"

Betty laughed. "How can you prove it?"

Shelly pulled a vial from her purse. Inside was a swirling potion that appeared as if ripe citrus fruits, peel and all, had been juiced, mixed with crushed pearls and dropped into the bottle. It reminded me of liquid sunshine. I wondered if it tasted the same.

"This is what I used to transform this man into a toad. It will also turn him back."

Betty scoffed. "And what's a potion going to prove? There could be anything in there."

Shelly nodded. "There could be. Unless I made it in front of you."

"Why would you make it in front of us?" Amelia said. "We might steal the recipe."

Shelly tipped her head. "You might. You might not. It's a risk I'm willing to take."

Betty pulled her corncob pipe from a pocket and lit the tobacco already packed inside. She blew a smoke square to the ceiling. "Why are you telling us this?"

Shelly poked the air with one bloodred fingernail. "Because I need the Craples. How about we work a little magic and I'll tell you everything?"

Betty opened her mouth, but Shelly cut her off. "Before you judge my potion, why don't you watch it? See for yourself I'm telling the truth."

Betty scowled. "Fine. Show us."

Shelly whipped the dome from the toad. The amphibian sat motionless as she uncorked the vial and tipped it, solution aiming for the creature. A single drop of potion splashed on the toad's back.

The witch smiled. "You can also take it by mouth, but it's hard to feed a toad."

Shelly placed the amphibian on the floor. Within seconds its back smoked. The fog thickened. Gray smoke filled my lungs. It tickled my throat. The four of us coughed. Not pretty, delicate throaty things. No, this was hacking, ugly coughs that you only do in the privacy of your bathroom.

From behind the smoke wall I heard snaps and cracks that, honestly, made me want to vomit.

As the fog cleared, I could easily make out something half toad/half human flopping on the floor. A few more seconds later and a young man sat beside Shelly.

He was fully dressed, I'd like to add. Not sure where the clothing came from, but I was glad for it.

"This is Bo," Shelly said.

Bo kissed her cheek. "So glad to be back, darling. As much as I enjoy a little change now and then, a toad is really a bit too much for me."

Betty's gaze darted to Shelly. "That proves nothing. Just because you used a potion doesn't prove blood wasn't worked into the mixture."

Shelly squinted. "It proves a potion brought him back. There was no sacrifice involved. No bloodshed. Surely even you can see that?"

Betty's brows hitched. "I won't believe it until I know every ingredient in that liquid and watch for myself as a person is transformed."

Shelly licked her lips. "I will show you how I make it. But I will only show you, and there's one caveat."

"Oh, here we go." Betty slapped her thigh. "Here's where the black magic comes in."

"No black magic," Shelly said in her buttery voice.

Bo cleared his throat. "Might I say something?" He didn't wait for anyone to agree. "I'm a wizard and don't dabble in darkness. I would never have agreed to do this unless Shelly proved to me that no sacrifice was involved. The old, arcane methods of transmuting humans to animal is over. Shelly has discovered a new way."

"What's the caveat?" Betty said. "The catch? What is it?"

Shelly's eyes glittered so brightly I was surprised she didn't rub her hands with glee. "The catch, as you call it, is that I will show you how I prepared the potion in exchange for a service."

"What service is that?" Betty said.

"I need a volunteer for my potion—at the contest. You understand I can use someone I've brought with me, but for the judging to be fully believed, it would behoove me to use a town local. Someone everyone in Magnolia Cove trusts."

All eyes turned to Betty.

Betty's voice soured. "You mean me."

"I mean you," Shelly said. "You're the most trusted person in this town. You must volunteer to be touched by the potion and then quickly turned back—I mean very quickly. You won't be a toad for longer than a few moments. Only then will I teach you the potion."

Silence filled the room. Betty's eye twitched. Here's the thing—Betty's original occupation was that of a witch pharmacist, or healer, for lack of a better description. So my grandmother by nature was someone who liked grinding and working with natural substances to cure people or change things—potion making, as it were.

So the fact that Shelly Seay dangled a potion that worked a curveball around black magic, or shot a hole through it, was like finding a diamond in a cave to Betty. Essentially Shelly had approached the exact right person for her bidding.

Betty's curiosity would be too much. She'd want to know all about the potion. She would have to. It was in her nature.

My grandmother blew another smoke square that floated to the ceiling and remained like mist. Her gaze darted around the room until it finally landed on Shelly.

The sorceress hitched a brow. "Well? Do you have an answer?"

"I've got an answer for you."

I held my breath.

"No," Betty said. "I will not under any circumstances help you with this potion. I don't believe you. Somewhere in this spell is dark magic —the work of using blood. I know it." Betty rose. "Now, it was wonderful visiting with you, but I would like it if you and your sorcering ways left."

Shelly's mouth twitched. "You're making a mistake."

The front door blew open. A wind whipped my hair until it covered my eyes. I pushed it aside.

Betty's eyes blazed with anger. Her shoulders tensed. Her mouth formed a thin line.

She pointed to the door. "I'm not making a mistake. I'm keeping one from being created."

Whoa. I didn't remember the last time I'd seen Betty so ticked. But still, Shelly and her boyfriend, or whoever he was, exited stage left.

Betty brushed her hands as if ridding herself of grime. "Well now that that's settled, what would y'all like to do for the rest of the day?"

I ALREADY HAD PLANS. Which was good because I didn't know how long Betty's nasty mood would last, and y'all, I didn't want to be anywhere near her.

So I headed on over to Axel's house to say goodbye to his parents.

His mother, Karen, wrapped me in a huge hug. "It's been wonderful meeting you, Pepper."

"You too." I inhaled the scent of vanilla and goodness that haloed her hair. "Where are y'all headed?"

Karen eyed their RV. "Florida. I like to go where it's warm in the winter."

"Can't say I blame you."

I gave Roger a hug while their new dog, Arsenal, yipped at my legs. I picked up the beagle and gave him a cuddle. "I'm going to miss you, boy."

Thank you, the dog said.

I scratched his head. "You're welcome."

Arsenal thanked me because I'd recently put the person who killed his mistress behind bars. That person had been his master. Since Arsenal was currently an orphan, he'd found a great family in Axel's parents. They were happy for the company, and the dog had new parents. It was a win-win.

Axel and I watched as his parents drove off, the RV rumbling as Roger steered it down the road.

Axel wrapped an arm around my shoulder. "You got your wish granted last night."

I certainly had. The wishing hat that sat atop a snowman had shot a slip of paper to me that revealed the secret Christmas wish I had made was granted.

I nuzzled my head to his shoulder. "So I did."

Axel's hand slid down my arm. His skin left a trail of fire burning over my flesh. I shuddered as a pulse of want flared in my body.

His breath tickled my ear as Axel whispered. "Are you going to keep your wish a secret? You can, you know. It's not as if you have to tell me."

I laughed. "Are you, Axel Reign, dying to know what I wished for?"

"No, no, not at all. But if I just thought you might like to tell someone. Get it off your chest."

I tipped my head back to meet his gaze. His blue eyes held light and love. One look sent a barb straight to my heart, pinning it to my spine and stealing my breath as well as my wits.

My tongue disappeared from my mouth.

In a good way. It was all in a good way.

I fingered the locket he'd given me for Christmas. Beautiful was an inept word to describe the protection locket. A golden vine snaked around the front. I loved it. Almost as much as I loved him.

"Okay, I'll tell you what I wished for."

Mischief sparked in his eyes. "Was it to win the potion-making contest?"

"Ha. No." I wove my arm through his as he guided us back inside his house. "I didn't wish for that, but the weirdest thing happened."

"Not in Magnolia Cove," he said with mock surprise.

I chuckled. "Oh, sir, you know this town too well."

"Very true."

He opened the door for me, and I slinked into the warmth. I sucked it up like a fish returned to the water. It felt so delicious.

"Anyway, this woman Shelly Seay showed up at the house today.

She'd worked some sort of transformation potion on a man that turned him into a toad."

"That's transmutation, and it uses dark magic."

"Tsk, tsk. You only think you know all the answers, Axel," I teased as I shrugged from my jacket. "She said she'd created a potion that didn't use any sort of black magic. Shelly wanted to prove it by showing Betty her recipe. But that came with a catch."

"What catch?"

I explained the rest of the situation. He listened silently, studying me.

When I finished, he drummed his fingers on the kitchen counter. "And Betty said no."

"Yes. She didn't want to have anything to do with it."

"Probably for the best."

"Why?"

Axel slid a hand over the dark stubble on his jaw. "I've heard of people trying to bypass black magic before with these sorts of spells. It never works."

My eyebrows shot up. "It doesn't?"

"No. It generally seems like a good idea, but when it comes right down to it, the potions are unstable. They don't hold. Either that, or they hold too long."

My mouth quirked in confusion. "What do you mean?"

"What I mean is, if Betty had drunk that potion, there's no guarantee in the stability of the solution. She could've been stuck as a frog forever."

THREE

*T*he next day life started getting back to normal. If you call magic exploding from people's chimneys normal, I guess.

A loud *crack* rang outside the house. The cottage rumbled and jolted. Picture frames tumbled to the floor. Knickknacks toppled over and splintered into fragments. I grabbed a nearby wall to steady myself.

"What's going on?" I shouted at Betty.

She waved her hand. The picture frames righted themselves and knickknacks sewed themselves together. "It's only the week before potion contest shenanigans. Folks lock themselves in their houses and nearly destroy their homes in order to perfect their potions."

The rumbling stopped. I brushed a curtain of hair from my eyes and slowly straightened. I wasn't sure if I should wait for another rumble or not. "Sheesh. I hope no one accidentally blows themselves up."

"Happens every year." Cordelia floated in and smiled nonchalantly.

My jaw dropped. "What?"

She dismissed me with a wave. "It's fine. No one ever gets hurt, but some come pretty close."

"This year," Amelia said, sailing down the stairs, "I'm going to win. I'm creating a potion to beat all potions."

"And what potion would that be?" Cordelia said.

Amelia smiled brightly. "One that makes even the grumpiest person happy for thirty minutes."

Betty, Cordelia and I stared at each other. No one said a word.

Amelia tapped her foot impatiently. "I know y'all think it's stupid, but here's the thing—if you've got to break bad news to someone, give them a drop of this potion and they won't be so mad."

"What about when it wears off?" I said.

"Oh, they'll be ticked then," Cordelia said.

"Okay, so I haven't worked out all the kinks." Amelia's face reddened. "Don't worry, I'll have all the wrinkles smoothed by the time it's contest day. Don't any of y'all worry."

Cordelia flicked her long blonde hair over one shoulder. "Don't worry. I won't."

"Sometimes I hate you," Amelia said.

Cordelia flashed her a huge grin. "But I love you."

Amelia grumbled something unintelligible.

"Girls," Betty interrupted, "I suggest the three of you get on your potion making if you're to enter the contest. From the sounds of outside, you're going to have some stiff competition."

Amelia plucked a biscuit from a dish and peeled it open. "And what're you going to be making this year?"

Betty tapped her nose. Her eyes glittered with delight. "That's for me to know and you to find out."

I ate and went upstairs. The week between Christmas and New Year's was a vacation week in the witch town. No one worked. Instead everyone spent their time making and perfecting—you guessed it, potions. Unless you were an overachiever, that was. I supposed if you aligned yourself with that particular coven, you were already set for the competition.

And that would not be me.

As I'd only just discovered that the contest was basically a rite of passage in Magnolia Cove, I was doing this whole thing by the skin of my teeth.

I opened the lid of the potion-making kit and stared at the vials and pouches of powder.

"Don't know what you're doing, sugarbear?"

I glanced over at Mattie the Cat, who was curled up on the windowsill. Hugo, my pet dragon, lay on the floor, his tail sweeping the rug in greeting.

"No, I have no idea what I'm doing. I could use about a million pounds of help."

Mattie stretched and jumped to the floor. She padded to the box, looked inside and sniffed. "First of all, this is great for basic potion making. If you want to create a cream that gives your worst enemy the boil of their life on their butt, this is what you'd be needin'. But if you want to actually make a potion that places, you can grab the vials and throw the rest of it out the window."

Her harshness hurt my feelings. "It's a starter kit." It came out a whimper. "I don't know anything about potion making."

"Sugarbear, I know all there is to know about it." She arched her back in what looked like an awesome stretch. "I can help you. Now." She sat on her haunches and blinked. "What is it you'd like to make?"

I frowned. "I have no clue."

"Okay, well think about things that move you."

"Amelia wants to put someone in a good mood for thirty minutes."

"She must be wantin' to give Cordelia or Betty bad news."

I tapped my foot. "There's a lot going on." I'd bought Axel wrist bands that should help us communicate when he's a werewolf. I was hoping to really break through to him.

"To knock the feral out?"

"Yep," I said. I rubbed my forehead. Heck, in a magical town like mine there were about a thousand ways I could go. But what was the most pressing at the moment?

"I want to stop chaos."

Mattie did the closest thing to laughing I'd ever heard. It was sort of cackle and meow—strange and grating. "Sugar, you've got chaos witches for aunts."

"That's not what I mean."

Quiet covered the room. "What do you mean?"

"Cordelia and Amelia's fathers are here. I'm afraid their dads are going to cause powers latent in my cousins to come forward. Powers that might be more detrimental than not. Because of their heritage. I want to stop that. Be able to put a hold on it."

Mattie peered again into the box. "Sugar, you're going to need a lot more ingredients than are in this box. The stuff you're going to need would belong to one person."

"Who's that?"

"A wizard."

"Axel, then."

"Yep. We'd better get over there if we're going to create the sort of potion you want to make."

"Let's go."

I packed up the box and led Mattie and Hugo to my riding cast-iron skillet. I hiked one leg over the pole. Mattie jumped on the front, and Hugo flew alongside us.

We'd made it just past Bubbling Cauldron when I noticed Shelly Seay walking through town. That wasn't the weird part. Walking beside her was Betty.

Betty!

What was Betty doing with Shelly?

I didn't have time to think because a whirl of magic whizzed past. A sphere flaring with power shot across the sky and splashed into a tree.

Another witch on a cast-iron skillet appeared beside us. It was a young woman with frizzy dark hair wearing long black robes.

"Get the dragon out of here," she yelled.

I dug my heels in and skidded to a stop. "What are you talking about?"

The little witch zoomed past. "My potion! It finds magical creatures and sticks to them like glue. It's a beacon. Your dragon is magical! The ball will find him."

The sphere pulled itself off the tree and shot straight toward us.

"What happens if it finds him?"

The witch scrunched up her face. "I don't know! I haven't figured that much out yet!"

That didn't sound good. "You'd better get us out of here," Mattie said. "Sounds like that witch don't know what she's doing."

I agreed. Time to get the heck out of Dodge. "Let's go, Hugo!"

I reached down and found a well of power ready to be tapped. My skillet zoomed on over the trees, and Hugo kept up. I glanced back to see the ball knock into the frizzy haired witch's chest. She somersaulted, and when the spinning stop, her chest was covered in magical goo.

Better her than us.

By the time we reached Axel's house, Hugo was out of breath and adrenaline zipped through me.

"Back so soon?" he said in greeting.

"I need your equipment."

His eyes bulged. "Excuse me?"

I rolled my eyes. "Your *magical* equipment. I need the powders and whatnot you have downstairs."

"Oh." He placed a hand over his heart. "As much as I would love to give you my equipment, I was sure that wasn't what you meant."

I fisted a hand against his arm. "You're right. It wasn't. I'm here to create the greatest potion ever known to mankind."

Axel gestured for me to enter. "Please don't let me stop you."

He led me downstairs. Mattie and I worked while Axel played upstairs with Hugo.

As I stood in front of the wall of vials and boxes, I realized something. "I don't think I want to make that potion. The one to stop the chaos."

"Then what do you want to do?"

I bit down on my lip. I wasn't sure if it would work. "I have an idea. I don't know if it's possible, but I'd like to try."

"What is it?"

"Well, you know how I made a wish in the hat this year?"

"I think I might've heard something about it." Mattie jumped on a shelf and licked her paw. "Course I don't know what it was about."

"Well the wish was that I could talk to Axel when he's a werewolf. The wish was granted."

"That's good."

"So I want to make a potion around that. Something to go with it."

Mattie nodded. "Okay. What're you thinking?"

I eyed bottles of ingredients I only knew in passing. "This is what I want to do."

FOUR

*T*he day of the potion making contest finally arrived. For the past days I'd been staying up late, waking up early and barely eating. I was determined to create a wonderful potion.

I knew what my cousins had said, that the rest of the world took New Year's very seriously so witches didn't when it came to potions, but I didn't care. My potion was serious stuff, and I was super proud of it.

I awoke stiff and sore. Hours of grinding and whisking had taken their toll. I yawned, took one look in the mirror and cringed.

It looked like Death had ridden a motorcycle over my face. My hair stuck out like hay, I had deep wells under my eyes and my skin looked dry to the point of cracking.

Mattie jumped from the windowsill. "You need some TLC, sugarbear."

I stretched a kink from my neck. "Ow. If I win today, I will personally make you a new pillow to lie on."

"I could use it." Mattie glanced at the clock. "What time are you supposed to be there?"

"Ten."

"It's nine thirty."

"Crap! I overslept." I jumped in the shower, slapped lotion all over my body and threw on some clothes. "Crap! Crap! Crap! Crap!"

Hugo stared at me with huge question marks in his eyes.

"I'm late, Hugo. Come on, y'all! Let's go."

"Pepper," Cordelia yelled from downstairs. "Are you coming?"

I opened my door. "Yes! Go without me. I'll catch up."

A few minutes later I shouldered my purse, threw on my coat and headed out the door.

"Wait," Mattie said. "Aren't you forgetting something?"

"What?" I dug in my heels to stop.

"The potions!"

I nearly fisted myself in the head. "Yes!"

I grabbed a box rattling with corked vials that were filled to their brims with purple liquid.

By the time I arrived at the contest, the whole town was there. Tables were set up all over the park across from Bubbling Cauldron. A grand judging table had been set up. A man in a white cravat and dark suit walked around like he owned Magnolia Cove.

Cordelia sidled up to me. "Saltz Swift."

I clutched my chest. "Ah! You about scared me to death's open door."

"I almost wish I had." She winked to let me know she was joking.

I leaned forward. My breath caught in my throat. Wait. She'd said *almost wish*. Not the same as a real, full-on wish. I relaxed.

"Where are y'all?"

Cordelia pointed to a table. "We're over there, but there isn't room. We tried to save you a spot, but it got snatched up. These witches are cray-cray."

Panic filled me. "Where am I going to set up?"

Cordelia nodded to a long table at the very front. The table I'd seen Saltz Swift parading in front of.

Ugh. I didn't exactly want to be under the potion master's nose, but what other choice did I have?

As my luck would have it, the only spot left was slap in the middle of the table. I set down my box clinking with vials and began unpack-

22

ing, same as everyone else. I set the potions out prettily but realized the other contestants had done some serious decorating.

Plenty of witches had placed pointy hats in front of their vials or they'd draped scarves over the surfaces. One even had little balls of magic circling overhead.

I mean, come on—little balls of magic? This was a potion contest, not a magical display.

And then there was me. All I had was a cardboard box and corked vials. Wow. I would've felt like an underachiever if I hadn't spent the past few days barely eating and resting to make my potion really stand out.

"And you are?"

The voice took me by surprise. I turned to see Saltz Swift staring down at me.

His creamy caramel-colored skin was a stark contrast to his ice-blue eyes. His dark hair was twisted into a pompadour at his crown. The man's aura was all masculine and power. He was seriously intimidating, and I figured he had more magic in his little pinky than I carried in my entire body.

I mean, that might not be true, but it was certainly the vibe oozing from him.

"I'm Pepper Dunn."

He leaned over the table and plucked one of the vials. "Betty Craple's granddaughter, I believe."

"Yes." I barely had breath in my lungs. I think Saltz had yanked all of it out with his mere presence.

"The familiar matcher."

"Yes, I do match familiars with their witches."

He dragged his gaze from the potion to me. "You should come to the school and give a lecture on it."

I did a double take. "I'm sorry?"

"Surely you know of our school—the Southern School of Magic."

Um. I hated to tell him, but I'd never heard its name.

It seemed Saltz was insulted by this knowledge. He replaced the vial with two fingers as if it had threatened to give him herpes. "I see your grandmother hasn't bothered to teach you some of the basics of our lives. That will need to be rectified."

Well excuse me.

"The Southern School of Magic is where all of us learned our craft." He eyed me up and down and sniffed. "At least for those of us who grew up knowing we were witches. If we don't receive our powers until we're older, then that's a different story."

"You're saying I'm a different story."

"Yes, exactly."

Well that's mighty rich of you.

He gestured to a vial. "I like how your potion is hiding in plain sight."

I frowned. "I'm sorry?"

"In your cardboard box, as it were. I wish some of the other contestants would consider hiding their potions since most of them are miserable failures."

"Oh." This Swift guy definitely didn't mince or chop or even shuffle words, did he? Said exactly what he thought.

"Tell me, what sort of potion do you have here?"

"Well, you see—"

"Potion Master, it's time for the judging to start."

A round man clasping a clipboard ran over to us. His curly mop of hair tumbled in his eyes as he hopped from one foot to the other. "Potion Master, time to start," he repeated.

"I know that, Anthony," Saltz snapped. "I was only talking to young Miss Pepper Dunn here." He leaned forward. His blue eyes twinkled. "It is Miss, isn't it?"

Ugh. I nearly vomited. The fact that he was coming on to me was seriously the most revolting thing that had happened to me in years.

Before I had a chance to answer, Saltz took my hand. "We'd love to have you at the school. For a lesson," he affirmed.

"You've got over two hundred potions to judge, Master," Anthony said impatiently.

"I know, Anthony. I'm coming." Saltz smiled. "I pray your potion is up to the test, Miss Dunn."

"I hope so."

Saltz frowned at Anthony. "It's only witches and wizards this year, I hope? No half bloods?"

My heart tightened. By half blood I'm sure he meant someone like Axel.

Jerk.

"Let me see." Anthony checked his clipboard as he whisked Saltz off, reciting a list of folks.

Axel's breath warmed my neck. "I see you were getting cozy with Swifty boy."

The scents of leather and musk drifted from Axel's flesh and trickled up my nose. This was as close to heaven as I would ever reach on earth.

I leaned my back onto his chest. "Thank goodness you've rescued me. I thought I was going to turn into slime just talking to him."

Axel laughed into my ear. His warm breath tickled my skin and made me smile. "No way you would ever turn into slime. Maybe you'd feel slimy and need a bath, but you wouldn't turn into it."

"Thank goodness."

I peeled off Axel and smiled widely. "I got it finished."

He glanced at the arrangement of bottles. "You going to tell me what it is?"

I shook my head. "Nope. It's a surprise. But I think you'll like it."

He rubbed my arms and smiled. "I'm sure I will." A thought crossed his face and his expression darkened to the point it nearly frightened me. "But listen, if Swift bothers you, tell me. He's known to be lecherous."

I quirked a brow. "Lecherous? Quite the word."

"I use it because it's true."

"And how would you know that?"

"Because I'm lecherous." The spark in his eyes confirmed Axel was joking, but I play punched his arm anyway.

"Saltz Swift asked me to speak at the school."

Axel slid his rear onto the table. Seriously, there was nothing sexier than watching him move. Thank you, Jesus, for creating Axel Reign and making him mine—all mine.

He grazed a thumb down his straight jaw. "Did he now? Wants you for the school?"

"He wants me to talk about familiars."

"Great idea. There should be a class or lecture taught on that. It's important."

I poked him. "Are you being sarcastic?"

"Absolutely not. Children should know the rules of familiars and how the animals play an integral part in each witch's magic. If anyone should teach them that, it should be you."

I rolled my eyes. "I hope you're joking. I barely know anything about familiars. I can match, but teaching someone how to use their animal is a different story."

"Don't sell yourself short."

My lips tipped to a smile. "How about I try not to?"

"Sounds perfect."

"Ladies and gentlemen."

Axel rose and I turned to the podium. Mayor Battle stood at a lectern, arms wide. "Allow me to welcome you to the one hundredth New Year's Potion Making Contest. Our illustrious panel of judges—" He pointed to two wizards and one witch. Beautiful loose curls swam around her face.

"And of course our primary judge, Potion Master Saltz Swift himself!" Mayor Battle pointed to the wizard, who tipped his head to the clapping crowd. "Let the judging begin!"

And so it went. Each contestant was supposed to bring their potion to the judges for inspection. The entire crowd could hear if not see what the contestants had created.

"I'm going to grab some food." Axel dug his hands into his pockets. "You hungry?"

"Yes. Starving."

"Great. There's a witch food truck just down the street. They serve the best eyeball stew you've ever tasted."

I think a croak escaped my lips.

"Kidding. They've got pulled pork barbecue sandwiches topped with cole slaw. Want one?"

"Yes. Dying for one."

"I'll be back." He kissed me swiftly on the lips and vanished through the crowd.

"Well well well, I see you've brought a potion."

I shivered as Shelly Seay sauntered toward me, towing her little dark-haired boy toy behind her. She wore a satin brocade dress that rustled like liquid fire.

Shelly stopped and turned. "The little witch who only recently became one of us decided that she could play with the big boys." She cocked her eyes wide. "Is that it?"

I narrowed my gaze at her. "Listen, just because my grandmother said she didn't want to have anything to do with your potion doesn't mean it's okay to insult me. I don't go around insulting you and your potions, do I?"

Shelly's crimson lips curled into a smirk. "You can try, little girl, but you won't be able to keep up with me. My potion will win this contest." She started to move on. Her man Bo practically wagged his tail as he kept up.

"Besides," Shelly added, "whoever said your grandmother isn't helping me?"

She cackled as she walked on. I opened my mouth to protest, but what was there to argue? I had seen Betty and Shelly talking several days ago. I'd just been so wrapped up in my own world of potions that I'd forgotten to ask my grandmother about it.

I should have. I definitely should have from the arrogant way Shelly talked.

"She's something, isn't she?"

The little witch that had nearly attacked my dragon with a magical ball the other day popped up in front of my table. She cocked her head toward Shelly.

"Shelly, I mean. Most people wouldn't allow a rumored sorceress at these things, but what do I know? I'm just a School of Magic flunky who likes to make potions."

I smiled. Even if she had almost hurt my dragon, the witch at least seemed nice. "I'm Pepper Dunn, and I'm not particularly fond of Shelly, either."

The witch extended her hand. Dark eyes like buttons peered out from under her mess of ebony hair. Freckles constellated her nose and cheeks, and her grin was big, wide.

"I'm Gale East. Like a wind. Like an easterly wind at that."

"Nice to meet you."

Gale eyed my table. "Good luck to you. I'd better get back to my own potion before someone tries to claim it as their own." She shrugged. "I don't know why they would, seeing as I barely managed to perfect it. But anyway, just wanted to give you some support for Shelly. She can be the worst. She used to teach at the school, you know."

"Oh, that's right. I'd heard that but don't know the story."

Gale leaned in conspiratorially. "Yep. Taught witch defense. Started out teaching potions, but then Saltz Swift got a job there and of course he's the potion master, so that's the job he got. For a while he and Shelly taught together."

Gale lowered her voice. "But from what I heard, they were having an affair and the school board got wind of it. So instead of either of them being fired, they moved Shelly to witch defense."

From my brief meeting with Saltz, I wasn't surprised at all.

"Anyway, I'd better get going. Glad the dragon's okay." Gale gave a quick wave and left.

I stood outside the rest of the day. You wouldn't believe how long it took for judges to go through two hundred plus entrants, but forever seemed an apt word to describe it.

By the time the sun burned down the horizon and the sky bled pink and gold, they'd arrived at Shelly Seay's entry.

"Ladies and gentlemen," Shelly announced to the crowd. Her bright red lips looked especially vivid even in the waning light. Must've been some sort of magic spell.

"Impressive," Axel said.

He was such an awesome boyfriend. Axel had spent most of the day keeping me company even though I was pretty much certain he was bored out of his mind.

The wind picked up. I rubbed the chill from my arms. "What's impressive?"

"The fact that Shelly's bringing the crowd into this. As you've seen, none of the other contestants have."

"Hmm."

Shelly raised her arms high. "Y'all are about to witness the most amazing feat. Tonight, I will transmute a person into an animal without the use of blood magic."

The crowd gasped.

"So dramatic," Axel murmured. I glanced at him. He winked at me. "Isn't it fun?"

I laughed. It was fun.

"For this," Shelly continued, "I'm using a volunteer from your very own town. Will all of y'all please welcome Betty Craple to the stage!"

My jaw dropped. My grandmother suddenly appeared beside Shelly. Betty's mouth was pinned in a frown, and her arms were folded across her chest.

Shelly held a vial high. "And now, I'm going to turn your beloved Betty Craple into a toad."

My stomach fell to China. My gaze crashed into Axel's.

"This should be interesting," he said.

I fisted my hands. Yep, it should be.

FIVE

*S*helly Seay held Betty's hand. "Tonight I will prove to y'all that transmutation can occur without the use of dark magic. That you don't need blood to create a potion that uses the dark arts."

"Sorceress," someone yelled from the crowd.

Shelly snorted. "I see some things don't change. The prejudice of the past is alive and well in Magnolia Cove."

"Shelly," Saltz Swift snapped, "this is highly against the contest protocol."

"No it isn't," she said. "I want everyone to see what I've created. I don't want only the panel of judges to witness my greatest achievement. I want all of Magnolia Cove to see that when I win the title of potion mistress, it will be well deserved."

Coals of anger burned in her gaze. "And for those naysayers out there, those of you who don't believe I've done what I say I have—fine. You don't have to believe me, a sorceress, as you say. But do believe Betty Craple. She's one of your elite, is she not? Someone that every single one of y'all respects and admires? If you don't believe me, believe her."

Shelly whirled. Her thickly brocaded dress flapped like crow feathers. "Betty, is what I say true?"

"It is," Betty stated. "What Shelly has achieved is not done by sorcery. It is true potion making. There is no blood magic here. I was a skeptic. Y'all know I'm a skeptic, but I've seen it with my own two eyes. What Shelly has achieved will bring magic into a new century."

I rocked back on my heels. "Wow. Betty didn't want to have anything to do with Shelly."

Axel squeezed my shoulder. "Something made her change her mind."

A strange smell wafted through the air. It reminded me of mud and sulfur. "Do you smell that?"

Axel nodded. "Yeah. I don't like it."

"Why not?"

Before he could answer, my attention was drawn back to Shelly. "One drop of this potion and Betty will become a toad. Another drop and she will return to normal."

"Shelly, this spectacle must be stopped." Saltz stomped over to her.

"Why? Because I'm about to change witch history forever? Saltz, you will want to see this."

She uncorked the vial and let one drop fall onto Betty's head. Luckily my grandmother was much shorter than Shelly.

A cloud of smoke hissed from Betty's crown. The fog enveloped her. All I could hear was the popping and cracking of joints and bones. It lasted several seconds, during which I held my breath.

My gaze snagged to Cordelia and Amelia. They shot me hopeless looks. I knew we were all thinking the same thing—what if something went wrong? And why the heck didn't Betty bother to tell us that she was going to go through with it? We would've liked to know that our grandmother had decided to be Shelly Seay's guinea pig in front of a crowd of hundreds.

You know, we liked being in the loop on these sorts of things.

But we probably would've tried to talk Betty out of it. I know we would have. My grandmother had her reasons for not letting us in on her secret. Her decisions were hers alone.

I was quickly reminded of that when the smoke cleared and Betty now squatted on the platform as a toad.

"Crooooaaaak!"

I fisted Axel's jacket in my hand. "I might faint."

"I'll catch you, but then I'll have to kiss you. Probably on the neck."

I laughed and watched the scene. That horrid smell trickled up my nose again. "What is that?"

Axel's brow pinched together. "It's some sort of magic. It's on the tip of my tongue, but I can't quite remember. I'll have it in a second."

"You said it wasn't good."

"It's not." He raked his fingers through his dark hair. "But I can't remember how."

"Behold," Shelly cried, "I've successfully transmuted a human into an animal without the use of blood magic and without the use of any glamours. This isn't an illusion. This is real."

The crowd gasped. There were some murmurs of sorcery, but mostly everyone seemed as shocked as I was.

"And now," Shelly announced, "I will return this toad to her normal state, and she can attest to the purity of my potion."

Shelly raised the vial. "Time to transmute!"

But then she stopped. She clutched her chest as if she was in pain. Shelly shook it off and held the glass container high once more.

"I will change her!" Shelly crumpled in half, bending at the waist as if in agony.

"The smell," Axel said.

"What is it?"

Axel grabbed my hand. "It's a shifting spell. It allows the user to use a poppet to bring harm to someone."

"A poppet?" I'd never heard of such a thing.

"A voodoo doll. Someone's trying to kill Shelly. Come on!"

Axel and I raced across the platform to the other side, trying to reach Shelly. Axel chanted under his breath. He lifted his free hand and gestured. The air shifted, and symbols and shapes lit the air. I'd seen him do that one other time, but never before that. It was like Axel's magic had changed after he'd left Magnolia Cove.

The crowd wove together. Axel and I fought to get through.

A thick black cloud erupted where Shelly stood. The crowd of witches gasped and recoiled. The smoke was so thick it was impossible to see. I coughed and gasped.

Axel yanked me through the crowd. By the time it cleared, we had reached Shelly Seay.

She lay motionless on the wooden platform, staring vacantly up at a sky that was quickly turning to twilight.

Betty, still in toad form, sat beside Shelly's limp body. Bo, Shelly's other half, draped himself over her.

"Shelly! Shelly!" He glanced upward. "No!"

I pressed my face against Axel's shoulder. It was impossible to not realize that Shelly Seay was very much dead. But that wasn't all.

The vial that would turn Betty to normal had disappeared.

SIX

*S*heriff Garrick Young got the scene contained quickly. He roped it off and made sure no one could escape while his officers searched madly for the potion vial.

But it was gone.

And by gone, I mean long gone.

No one could locate it.

The officers spread out and questioned everyone on the scene, but it appeared as if the vial had up and vanished at the same time that Shelly Seay had been murdered.

Yes, murdered.

Axel and I stood off to the side. I was holding Betty in toad form. She blinked up at me with her yellow eyes as if to say, *When in the blazes is someone going to change me back?*

"As soon as we can." I swiped a finger over her head. "We'll change you as quickly as possible."

Garrick strode by. He was tall and lean and wore the usual outfit of the Magnolia Cove police, which started with a wide-brimmed fedora, though Garrick's was battered and worn. He also wore a vest, dark jeans and cowboy boots. All the other officers wore leather dusters. It appeared Garrick had left his at home.

"Young," Axel said.

Garrick tipped his hat to us and stomped over. "What in hell's bells happened here, Reign? I've got a woman dead for no reason and a potion missing. For God's sake, this is a potion contest, not a blood magic one."

Axel's gaze swiveled from side to side to make sure no one was listening. "Someone used a poppet."

Garrick's eyes nearly popped from his head. "A poppet? Are you sure?"

"It's been a long time since I'd smelled the scent, but there was no doubting it. Sulfur and earth. Pepper caught whiff of it, too."

I nodded. "Course I didn't know what it meant, but I smelled it."

Garrick tapped his fingers on his hips. "This ain't good."

"No, it isn't," Axel said. "Someone used a poppet, and if I had to guess, they crushed Shelly's heart."

"We'll do an autopsy." Garrick scratched his jaw. "You don't happen to know of anyone who uses them, er, poppet thingies, do you?"

Axel shook his head. "No one I'm aware of."

"Sure would make the investigation easier if you did."

"Sure would. But I don't."

Garrick nodded. He took a couple steps back. "If you hear of anything, let me know. I'll be investigating."

Axel tipped his head. "So will we. We've got a woman stuck in a frog's body, in case you hadn't noticed."

Garrick's gaze shifted to Betty. "We're looking for the potion, Ms. Craple. We'll find it."

As soon as Garrick left, I grabbed Axel's shirt. "That's what they wanted. The potion."

"Most likely. Shelly probably kept it under lock and key. This was the killer's only opportunity to snag it, so they did." His jaw clenched. "There's over two hundred people here. Two hundred witches. That's a lot for Garrick to sift through."

A sly smile tugged on my lips. "You thinking what I'm thinking?"

He nodded. "Let's start talking to folks."

Bo sat at a table, a blanket thrown over his shoulders. Poor guy was probably in shock.

"Hey, Bo," Axel said as we approached. "I'm sorry about Shelly."

Bo nodded sadly. "She was my everything. I would've transmuted into a worm for her."

"Course you would've wanted to come back," I said knowingly. "No one wants to stay a worm forever. I mean, that doesn't sound like a very good life. All you'd be doing is sifting through dirt, doing worm things. Ew. Definitely not fulfilling."

Bo said nothing. I guess my joke was lost on him. Perhaps now was not the time for jokes.

"Listen," Axel said, "Shelly turned you into a frog, right?"

"Toad," Bo corrected.

Axel pressed his foot into the leg of a chair. "Toad. Right. Sorry. But she did, didn't she?"

"Yes," he said stiffly.

In one fluid movement, Axel sat in a chair across from Bo. Bo's gaze flickered to Axel as if he was mostly bored and Axel seemed to just barely catch his attention.

"Here's the thing." Axel leaned in. "Whoever killed Shelly took the potion that will turn Betty Craple back to her true form."

"A short, angry woman?" Bo said.

I stifled a laugh. Betty as the toad glared at me. I transformed the laugh into a yawn. "So tired. Hard to believe how tired I am."

Axel rapped his knuckles on the table. "We need to return Betty, which means we've got to find that potion. Unless," he emphasized the word, "you know the ingredients."

Bo raked his fingers through his spiky hair. "Sadly, I do not know how Shelly constructed the potion. I never watched her. It was top secret." He pointed to the toad. "Betty knows. She watched. But as for anyone else with the knowledge—that's it. Just those two."

Axel rubbed his jaw. The answers he *wasn't* getting weren't helpful. "Where were you when Shelly died?"

Bo pointed to a spot on the stage. "Beside her."

"That's right," I said. "I remember seeing you. Bo, you wouldn't happen to know of anyone who wanted to hurt Shelly, do you? Anyone at all?"

Bo rubbed his sagging face. He looked exhausted, poor guy. "You heard what happened when she took the stage. People hated her. They called her a sorceress. If you want to find out who or what killed her, I suggest you start by talking to the people here."

Axel leaned back in the chair and smoothed his hands down his jeans. The sun had set, but someone had lit orbs of witch lights around the park. It was also unseasonably warm, thanks to a spell by some of the locals. It meant we could stay outside a little while longer. After all, it was January.

"One last question," Axel said.

"Yes?" Bo raked his fingers through his hair.

"Know anyone who uses poppets?"

Bo threw his head back and laughed. "Poppets? You've got to be kidding." But when Bo searched Axel's very serious face and found Axel not to be joking at all, his expression sobered.

"I don't know anyone who uses them." Bo cracked his knuckles. "That's such old magic and never taught anymore that I don't know the first thing about it."

"It's easy enough to find if you want to learn about it," Axel said.

"I'm sure, but it's not the sort of craft I've ever been interested in." Bo leaned forward and stared at Axel. "But if you're asking me who you should question next, the most likely person who would know about something like a poppet would be Saltz Swift, the potion master himself."

"Why him?" I absentmindedly stroked Betty's toad head.

Bo's gaze flashed to me. "Because for one, he teaches at the school. He would have access to all sorts of old spell books. I'm sure plenty of them would discuss poppets, even if they aren't taught. The other thing is that he was jealous of Shelly."

"He was?" That was news to me.

Bo nodded. "Desperately jealous of her. When he stole her position, all the kids hated him. They despised his method of teaching. He was never able to garner their respect like she did. So he hated her."

"Who'd you hear that from?" Axel said.

"Shelly."

I almost rolled my eyes. Of course the person who was kicked from her job would then turn around and spew that the new guy was hated. It sounded more like Shelly was jealous of Saltz than Saltz was jealous of Shelly. Besides, Saltz still taught at the school. And what about their supposed affair? Where was that information?

"Was Shelly still teaching somewhere?" I said.

"She tutored privately," Bo said. "She left the school a couple of years ago. They had moved her to teaching witch defense, and she didn't enjoy it as much."

Axel rose. "Thank you, Bo. I appreciate your help."

"Anything else I can tell you, let me know," Bo said. "I need to know what happened to Shelly. I loved her."

"We want to turn Betty back into Betty," I said.

Bo's gaze flickered to the toad in my palms. "I wish I could help you, but like I said, I don't know the potion. But I tell you what—I'll look through Shelly's things and make sure she didn't leave a second vial somewhere. If she did, I'll bring it to you."

Axel handed Bo a business card. "Here's my number."

We left Bo and headed back to collect my box of vials. The park had thinned out, only leaving smatterings of people here and there. They were doing as I was about to—collect their potions and go. All of them. And one person had the potion we needed.

But where were they and who were they?

"Axel." I felt a bubble of fear rise in my chest.

"Yes?"

"What are we going to do about Betty?"

He was silent. Silence was never good. It didn't bode well for what he would say next, so it was no surprise when his next words were, "I don't know."

I cringed. "That's a horrible answer. That's like saying maybe we'll figure it out."

"It's not a maybe." His fingers slid over my palm. "We will figure it out. It'll be fine. We'll get Betty back to normal."

"Are you sure?"

He stopped walking. I stopped. He turned me to face him. A strand of hair fluttered over my eyes. I really needed shorter bangs.

He brushed it away. "We will solve this. I have lots of spell books that can help."

I grimaced. "But it wasn't a spell that did this. It was a potion."

"Have you tried talking to Betty?"

Wow. What a way to turn the tables. "No," I admitted. "I haven't even thought about it."

"Try," he said gently.

I stared at the toad and closed my eyes. I didn't have to close them, but I thought it might help.

Betty? Betty, are you in there?

Silence greeted me.

Betty, can you talk to me? We need to recreate the potion that Shelly used to transform you. Can you help us?

Silence.

Do you know the recipe?

I waited, listening for any blip or even a whisper. I focused so hard I thought I might pop a blood vessel. She had to be in there. I mean, Betty could jibber jabber with the best of them. There had to be part of her that could communicate with me. Just had to be. I knew she was there. All I had to do was listen.

But still nothing.

I wanted to scream. I wanted to throw things. We had to help my grandmother. There was no telling where Shelly's potion had gotten to. It could be in another state by now.

If there was one thing I'd learned about magic, it was this—the best way to break a spell was to use the original spell to do it. Trying to meddle with someone else's magic was difficult. Meaning, trying to break a spell someone else had cast was next to impossible.

And working around it was even worse.

We needed the original spell like nobody's business. To do that, I needed Betty to talk.

Talk to me! Betty, you've got to talk to me or else we can't help you!

I waited a few more seconds and then exhaled. My shoulders slumped, and I wanted to sink onto the ground and melt. Anything would be better than facing what I was about to admit.

Anything.

Axel rubbed my shoulders. "Well? Do you have an answer?"

"Yeah, I've got an answer." I didn't even try to hide the bitterness in my voice. "I've got an answer and it isn't good."

"What is it?"

"I can't hear Betty." My gaze locked on Axel's. "I can't hear her so we can't create the potion. She's trapped as a toad unless we can recover it."

SEVEN

*A*xel took me, my box of vials and Betty home. "I'll search through my books tonight and see if I can find anything that will help her."

I nodded. It was the only response I could muster. I was numb. This day had started out rough and had gone horribly wrong.

"Okay," was all I managed.

Cordelia and Amelia had taken Hugo and Mattie home, which was good because it was late. I trudged up the porch steps, barely greeting Jennie the Guard-Vine. The plant gave the toad a good sniff before unwinding to allow us in.

A tall man with gray hair greeted me upon entering. I immediately recognized him.

"Hello. I'm Bean—Ben Vink. Bean's my nickname."

"Pepper Dunn." I set the box on a table and plucked Betty out. "Where's Amelia?"

My cousin entered from the kitchen. "Oh, Pepper, you're home."

"Where's Cordelia?"

Amelia hitched a shoulder. "Upstairs. My dad heard about what happened and called."

"I wanted to stop by, make sure the girls were all right." Bean slid his fingers through his hair. "My brother wanted to come as well, but after Cordelia's initial reception…well, he decided to wait it out."

By initial reception he meant frigid response. Cordelia had made absolutely no bones about the fact that she wasn't the least bit interested in getting to know her father. She could care less about him.

In Cordelia's mind, her father had abandoned her. According to her mother, however, that wasn't exactly what had happened.

But it wasn't my place to throw myself in the ring and get involved.

Amelia's gaze lit on the toad. "Is that…?" She gasped. "Is that Betty?"

I nodded. "Sure as silk it is."

"Oh no." Amelia lifted the toad from the box. "How are we going to turn her back?"

I shook my head sadly. "I don't know. We don't have the potion. Axel went home to work something out. He's hoping he can find something in one of his spell books."

"Let's hope." Amelia nibbled her bottom lip. "Where would the town be without her?"

I shook my head. Tears pricked my eyes. I had no words. None.

"Well, she never liked me," Bean said. "Amelia told me what happened to her, but I was hoping she'd be back to normal when you returned. Even though she didn't care for me when I was younger, I had hoped she'd mellowed with age."

"Betty mellow?" I said. "You must be thinking of another Betty Craple."

Bean chuckled and rose. "It was nice seeing you, Amelia, but I should be off. Pepper, nice to have met you, officially."

Amelia gave her father a stiff hug, and he left.

As soon as he was gone, I turned to her. "Are you crazy? Did Cordelia know he was here?"

Amelia shook her head. "I made sure she was asleep."

"You mean you spelled her."

"Not exactly. Just made her some tea that might or might not make her tired."

"You know how she feels about her dad and uncle. She would've roasted him alive if she'd caught him here."

Amelia threw up her hands. "And what about me? Don't I get a say-so?"

"Yes, you do. But I suggest you meet up with him somewhere other than here—at least until Cordelia's anger calms so it's more like ashes instead of a full-on wildfire."

"They're my dad and uncle, too."

I raised my hands in surrender. "I know that. I'm only trying to help." I raked my fingers through my hair. It was all so frustrating. I wanted to strangle the air.

My gaze settled on Betty. "Anyway. This isn't what we need to focus on. We've got Betty here. Betty as a toad. Let's make her comfortable for the night. Get her some water, dirt, a box. Whatever she needs."

"She can sleep with me," Amelia said.

"I'll get her some food from the shop tomorrow. Crickets and whatever else I think she might like."

Both of us stared at Betty. Amelia spoke first. "Think we'll be able to break the spell?"

I sucked on my lips. "I hope so. For all of Magnolia Cove's sake, I hope so."

I AWOKE the next morning to a pair of yellow eyes staring at me. "Ah!"

I bolted up and nearly fell off the bed. Somehow Betty the Toad stay glued to my sheets. When my heart calmed, I picked her up and laid her on the edge of the bed.

"Okay, Betty, I get it. You need to be changed back to normal. Let's go downstairs and see what's going on."

I tugged on a pair of house slippers, scooped up Betty and was followed by my Dr. Doolittle gang of Hugo and Mattie. Cordelia and Amelia were already downstairs eating a breakfast of cold cereal and fruit.

"I hope she didn't scare you," Amelia said. "When I saw her climbing the stairs, I figured she was heading for your room."

I pushed away a rogue strand of hair sticking in front of my vision. "And you didn't bother to stop her."

Amelia smiled brightly. "I thought you liked surprises."

"Ha-ha. Yes, you know I love waking up to a toad on my chest."

"Me too," Cordelia said. "But anyway, what's the word on changing her back?"

"I'm going to head over to Axel's in a little bit and see what he's discovered. Hopefully something because Shelly's potion is gone and Bo doesn't know the recipe."

"But Betty should." Cordelia spooned cereal into her mouth. "That was part of the deal, right? Shelly showed Betty the potion, and Betty became her guinea pig." Her gaze flashed to Betty. "No offense."

Obviously Betty couldn't answer.

"I can't hear Betty." I exhaled a deep breath and steeled myself for their responses.

Cordelia grimaced. "That is bad."

"Definitely not good," Amelia said.

I grimaced. "I know. Oh, before I forget, Axel said a poppet was used to kill Shelly."

Amelia and Cordelia exchanged glances.

"What?"

"Did you say poppet?" Cordelia said.

"Yes. Why? I mean, I understand that sort of magic isn't worked very often, but that's what Axel believed it was."

"It's not worked very often," Amelia explained, "because in most towns it's illegal."

A wave of realization punched me in the gut. "Of course it is. Why would anyone allow the use of poppets? You could easily kill people."

"Exactly," Cordelia said. "So it's illegal." She cocked a brow. "Is Axel sure?"

I nodded. "I think so. We both smelled some sort of sulfur weird scent. It took him a few minutes to place it, but once he did, it was a poppet, he said. And didn't you see what happened to Shelly? It looked like a random heart attack and then some magical backfiring or something, and the next thing you know she's dead and the potion is stolen. So anyway, you know of anyone who might or might not have any experience with poppets?"

My cousins exchanged a long glance, and then Cordelia turned to me. "I think we do."

∽

I REACHED Familiar Place and made my way over to the aquarium where I kept the crickets. I cringed as I watched the little black insects hop and climb over one another.

These were food for other familiars. Betty had to eat. She couldn't live off biscuits and gravy in the state she was in. But instead of scooping out a handful of crickets, I decided the best approach would be quite the opposite.

I opened the lid and let Betty drop in. That way, she could eat till her heart's content.

Which, from the looks of her flying tongue, it appeared she was going to do.

I turned around and shrieked. Saltz Swift had slithered into my shop without me hearing even the tiniest rustle of his clothing.

"Good morning, Familiar Mistress."

Um. Okay. I wasn't exactly into titles, but whatever. I also wasn't into creepy men appearing in my shop as if they'd popped out of cloud of smoke.

"I'm not so sure it's a good morning, Master Swift."

He strode over to a chair and sat with a flourish. "Nonsense. Every morning I'm alive is a blessing, and thus a good morning."

I folded my arms and crossed to him. "It's not a good morning for Shelly Seay or my grandmother."

"So it isn't." His face pinched tightly. "But nevertheless, it is still glorious and the new witching year is upon us."

"So it is." I mean, what else was I supposed to say? Really?

"Have you considered my offer?"

45

"Your offer?"

"The one to come to the school and teach a lecture or two on familiars."

I almost slapped my forehead. "Yes! That offer. Of course. Actually, I haven't had a chance to consider it given that my grandmother's a toad and Shelly Seay was killed"—I studied him closely—"most likely by a poppet."

Saltz coughed so hard he nearly toppled from the chair. "A poppet! Are you out of your mind?"

"I am not out of my mind. There were traces of evidence that a poppet was used."

He scowled. "And what sort of evidence do you have?"

Well none. But I wasn't going to say that. Seemed Saltz got pretty riled at my mention of a poppet. Interesting.

"There's expert opinion—not me, I'm not an expert. But someone else."

He rubbed his chin. "Hmm. So someone else suggests dark magic was used to kill a witch, and you automatically believe them?"

I narrowed my gaze. "It is a very reliable source."

"Ah, I see. A very reliable source." Sounded like he didn't believe me. "My dear, you are new to witchcraft, so I will give you a few tips."

"Please do." I didn't want tips at all.

"The first is that poppets are illegal in most cities."

"I've heard."

He poked the air. "The second is that not many witches know how to use poppets. Not many at all. If someone did, you would have to question where they might have learned such dark and devious craft."

"I heard you've got some old witchcraft tomes."

He coughed and sputtered. Saltz plucked a handkerchief from his pocket and covered his mouth. "So I do. So do most witches. And it's true I work at a school with a library that may have books on the subject. But I can assure you the magic we teach at the Southern School is not geared toward creating evil witches. That's not what we do. We train witches for the world they will work and live in."

He plucked his collar to standing. "But anyway, if you're so keen on following the poppet theory, there are books at the library."

He rose with the same sort of flourish that he had sat with. "I'm sure if you wanted to know more on the subject, Keating's *Book of Spells* would be a good place to start. Lots of old potions and enchantments in there."

I made a mental note of the title. "And this one is at the library?"

Saltz nodded. "It is. You can check out the school. See the place where you'll be lecturing next semester." He smiled smugly. "We'd love to have you, Pepper Dunn." His gaze bounced around the shop. "Your…expertise in this area will be welcome." He paused and smiled. "At least by me."

With that, he left. I mumbled his last words. "At least by me. What in the world does that mean?"

I remembered that I'd stuck Betty in a tank to eat crickets to her heart's content. I glanced at the aquarium and noticed her bulging sides. She definitely looked plumper than when I'd dropped her in.

I pulled her out and settled her on the desk. "You look fat and happy, if not amphibious."

She blinked her yellow eyes.

"Sorry. Come on. Let's see if Axel's found anything about the spell. Maybe he's discovered a way to change you back."

I put her in a box and headed out the door. Before I locked up, I muttered, "Because I really don't want to go to that school."

Saltz insinuating that I wouldn't be welcome by anyone but him didn't sit well with me. I didn't know what I was worried about. It wasn't like I had to give a lecture.

But there was something in the potion master's eyes that said otherwise. It suggested I didn't have a choice. One way or another Saltz would get me into that school to teach.

But what would I find once I arrived? The thought was enough to pretzel my stomach in knots.

"Come on, Betty." It was best to distract myself. "Let's go see what Axel discovered."

EIGHT

"Ihaven't been able to find a good spell to transform Betty back."

I sat in Axel's kitchen. Betty sat in her box, blinking at us.

"When you say *good* spell, does that mean you've found bad spells?"

A smile tugged on his luscious lips. Kissable lips. *Stop it, Pepper.* I couldn't sit here and think about kissing Axel when Betty was in trouble.

I had to focus.

He wagged a finger. "You're smart. Yes. I've found plenty of dark spells that require someone to shed blood in order to return Betty to her original form."

I squinted. "When you say shed blood, do you mean just a little?"

Let's face it—if a spell only called for a thimbleful of the stuff, I could do that. I could donate a little plasma for a good cause. Heck, I'd done it when I was a normal person and not a witch. I'd given to the bloodmobile on more than one occasion.

I could do it again. After all, donating blood saved lives.

Axel shook his head. Dark hair brushed his shoulders. "It's not the amount that matters, it's the debt you incur by working the magic."

"Debt? To who? Like the grim reaper? To Betty? I don't like the sound of that word—debt."

Nope. It did not taste good at all.

"It's a debt to dark forces. When you use blood sacrifice, dark forces of magic, evil forces help with the spell. The wielder, often a sorcerer, then owes a debt to dark spirits—demonic in some cases. That's not the sort of magic we want to get involved in."

"No, it isn't."

We stood in silence, studying one another.

"If only there was a way to reach Betty." I stroked her head. "If she could communicate with us, then she could tell us the spell."

"But she isn't."

"She can't, I don't think." I chewed the inside of my lip. Was there a way to reach her?

I snapped my fingers. "Axel, the animal communication bands I gave you for Christmas. I have a pair, too. Do you think I could secure them to Betty and then I could hear her? Connect with her?"

For Christmas I had given Axel a pair of cuffs that could help us communicate when he was a werewolf. Hopefully that simple line of communication would be strong enough that Axel could fight the beast that dwelled within him and remain himself even when he was trapped in the creature's body.

He scrubbed a hand down his jaw. "Those cuffs are to bind the two people when they're human so that when one becomes an animal, they can hear each other. What I'm afraid of is that we can't hear Betty because she's completely animal."

A record scratched in my head. "Wait. What? You think Betty's gone completely animal?"

"You can't hear her, Pepper," he said gently.

I pointed to the box. "It's not as if she's trying to escape. So there must be some of Betty in there." I stared at the toad. "Even if we can't talk to her."

Axel opened the fridge and pulled out a gallon of sweet tea. He poured a glass and slid it over. Then he nudged a sugar bowl toward me. I uncapped the porcelain lid and found a rainbow of jellybeans.

"Thanks."

"You're welcome."

I plopped a few in the glass and waited for them to dissolve before drinking.

Axel pulled himself onto the counter and sat. "The thing about those cuffs is the connection works when both parties can already hear each other. When one person then shifts into an animal, the connection strengthens."

I thought about my wish from the hat being granted. I would be able to communicate with Axel when he was a werewolf. But it was more than that—my wish had been that Axel could be tamed. It was the one thing I wanted—for him not to be *enslaved* by the beast, but to own it.

Perhaps that was the curse of the werewolf and couldn't be broken.

No. I didn't believe that. Not for one minute. Axel could own himself. That's what the wish had meant when it was granted. That he would retain his humanness.

Because right now when he turned, he was anything but human.

I shivered.

"What's wrong?"

"Nothing." I sipped my tea. "Mmm. Delicious. But anyway, are you saying I couldn't band Betty and talk to her?"

"I don't know. Maybe. I'll have to research it."

I hitched a brow.

"I'm in territory I don't understand here. There are other wizards I can consult, but most of them have the exact same resources I do. Besides, while I was gone I did more training."

"You did? You haven't mentioned it."

"It was very personal."

I made a gesture that I didn't want to get in his personal business. "You don't have to tell me."

"It's okay. I went looking for myself and found it."

"Sounds like a spiritual quest."

"It was." Long pause while I held my breath. "I met a shaman."

"Whoa. A shaman? Like where you sat in a sweat lodge and smoked from a pipe sort of shaman?"

He smiled shyly. "Sort of like that, yes. Anyway, my magic deepened and I learned some things."

I cocked a brow. "Sounds very mysterious."

"If you only knew." He slid from the counter and rested beside me at the bar. Axel threaded his fingers through my hair. "Everything I learned was useful and good. Obviously." He took my hand and kissed the inside of my palm before entwining his fingers in mine.

"Yes," I said breathlessly. Axel closed in until he was within kissing distance. "But we're talking about Betty."

His lips traced my jaw. "So we are. We can still talk like this."

My groin stirred. "It's best we don't."

Axel drew away, and my mouth immediately yearned for him. He was lifesaving air suddenly yanked from me. Being denied him was true suffering—at least for me, y'all.

The toad made a weird throaty sound. My gaze darted down. Seriously though, talking or no, I couldn't make out with Axel in front of Betty.

That was gross.

I pushed a strand of crimson hair from my face. "So you'll research the bands?"

He nodded. "I will."

I snapped my fingers. "All that talk of research made me forget."

"What's that?"

"Saltz Swift came by the store when I was feeding Betty."

"You've got my attention."

I leaned toward Axel, who tucked a tendril of hair behind my ear. "Well, even Amelia and Cordelia said if anyone knew about poppets, it would be him. So I asked him."

"Of course you did. And what did the potion master say?"

"He was insulted."

"As he would be. That guy thinks highly of himself."

I laughed. "So he does. You think highly of yourself."

Axel chuckled. A spark flared in his eyes. "Not that highly."

"Anyway, he seemed pretty upset about the whole poppet thing, but he said if there was one book that covered poppets, it was Keating's *Book of Spells*."

Axel threw back his head. "Ah, yes. It's an old tome. It's not taught in schools because it's pretty racy."

"Racy? Like are there naked pictures inside?"

He laughed. "Not that kind of racy. It's got old spells, some of which caused harm to the caster. They backfired."

"Ew. Not good."

"No, but if you want to learn some arcane stuff, it's in Keating. Maybe we should take a look at it."

"Take a look?"

Axel's gaze darkened. "Yep. Let's see who checked it out last."

"How do we get to the school?"

Axel and I sat in his old Land Rover on the other side of Magnolia Cove. The one entrance I'd ever used in town was tree-lined and gorgeous. Right now I was staring at a train tunnel. It looked abandoned with leaves piled up at the entrance.

"We drive through there."

My expression twisted to disbelief. "You're kidding? That place looks like scary monsters are inside."

He laughed. "The Southern School of Magic is in its own place, to keep the kids safe from outsiders. We drive through the tunnel and we've arrived."

"Are you sure? Am I going to need a tetanus shot to go through?"

"Trust me and hold on."

Axel headed into the tunnel. It was black as tar. The vehicle lurched as we hit what felt like giant potholes.

"Why are there potholes in here?"

"They're magical. Like stepping stones. When we exit, we'll be in another place. It's not Magnolia Cove anymore."

"Where is it?"

Light split the tunnel. I shielded my eyes. When I opened them, we were outside the blackness. I glanced right and left and noticed two tunnels on both sides of us.

Axel noticed me looking. "Those are shortcuts from other magical towns. Magnolia Cove isn't the only place that filters into here."

I looked up and saw a giant brick plantation-style mansion on top of a lush green hill. A forest butted up against the back of the house. It reminded me of the Cobweb Forest.

"Looks like our forest," I murmured.

"It is. The Cobweb Forest is a strange beast. The woods wind into many places."

"So could you take the forest and end up here?"

"If it let you," Axel said mysteriously.

"That's cryptic."

He smiled and pulled into a parking spot. "So's the forest. It's a living, breathing thing that's hard to decipher."

"But it's where you go the nights you change." I didn't understand this conversation at all.

"Only because it lets me. The hillbilly giants live beyond it and we can find them, but only because the forest lets us."

I shivered. "I might need to stay away from the forest."

He hitched a brow. "Sounds like a great idea."

I followed Axel inside. It looked exactly like a house on the outside and on the inside, too. But it was much larger inside than out. Antique rugs, dark wood and winding staircases greeted us.

"This place reminds me of a castle more than a house."

Axel took my hand. "Just don't get lost."

"I'll try not to."

A few students passed by. There weren't many of them as it was the holidays. I didn't imagine lots of kids stayed at the school during the break, but there were a few.

They each wore a basic dark school uniform with an insignia on the sweaters. Axel led me past them down a hall into a two-story room that could've easily swallowed Betty's entire house.

Books lined the walls on both levels, but I didn't see any ladders to reach them.

We found the circulation desk. A small, mousy woman in a bright green sweater and wearing red-framed glasses was muttering to herself.

"She always gets the holidays off. I never do. I swear for one year…"

Axel cleared his throat. "Ahem."

The woman blinked up at us. Her gaze landed on Axel, and her eyes flared. Of course they did. Axel had that effect on women everywhere he went.

I mean heck, he had that effect on me, too.

"Oh my goodness," she said. "I didn't see you there." She glanced at me. "I didn't see you, either. Oh, and you've got a box. How wonderful. Are you selling something?"

It took me a moment but I recognized her as one of the judges from the panel. This mousy librarian was the woman who'd had that wonderfully teased-out hair. Now it was pulled back and not nearly as wild or lush, but either way, here she sat.

"Maybe you can help us," Axel said.

"I will most certainly try." She batted her lashes at him. "What can I do for you?"

"We're looking for Keating's *Book of Spells*."

The woman blanched. "Keating's *Book of Spells*? Are you sure? There are so many other wonderful tomes here at the library." She twiddled a pencil between her fingers. "We have books on magic work that aren't nearly as um, *controversial* as the Keating."

Axel's lips curved into a smile. When he made that expression with his blue eyes shining, it was hard for any woman to resist his desires.

I will yell hallelujah to firsthand experience there.

"Actually, there may be something else you can do. We need some help with transmutation."

I pointed to the box. The librarian rose and peered inside. "Oh my goodness! This is the toad that Shelly Seay created, isn't it?"

I nodded. "Yes. Weren't you one of the judges?"

The woman smiled proudly. "As a matter of fact, I was." She extended a hand. "Babs Cantrill."

After Axel and I introduced ourselves, Babs led us on a tour through the library. "It's a pity about the contest being canceled. I so look forward to it every year. But you know you can't exactly continue with a contest after someone's been killed." She leaned over and whispered, "It doesn't look good, you know. Oh, I know what people say, the show must go on and all that, but I have a hard time buying it when someone winds up dead."

"Murdered," I corrected.

Babs's eyebrows shot to peaks. "Murder? Is that what they're thinking?"

I glanced at Axel. He shrugged. "I don't think it's any big secret, but yes. That's what the police are pursuing."

"What a shame." She pointed left. "Over here you'll find our section on spell work. Most of it is very light seeing as we do teach youngsters, but there are some darker spells. The Southern School of Magic has the most comprehensive magical library in all the South."

She smiled widely. "We pride ourselves in it. I've spent years studying potions. That's how I came to be a judge." She sniffled. "Shelly was a controversial character, but she was liked by a lot of people."

Axel and I exchanged a look. "Did you like her?" I said.

"Oh yes," Babs said, almost sounding flustered. "We had coffee all the time. We'd discuss potions. She was an accomplished potion maker, but that's obvious from what she was going to reveal." She glanced at the box. "Or did reveal. I assume you're looking for a spell that will change this one back to her normal state?"

"Yes," Axel murmured, "among other things."

Babs pointed to the rows and rows of books. "I can recommend something if you don't find what you're looking for in"—she shuddered—"the Keating."

"That would be great." Axel shifted the box holding Betty. "Were you here when Shelly taught at the school?"

"Oh yes, I've been here for forever it feels like." She giggled. "Yes,

Shelly was very controversial. She and Saltz didn't get along at all. It was all-out war between those two." Her eyes misted. "But then I suppose they found common ground. Don't we all need common ground every once in a while?"

I nodded. "I suppose we do. So did they um, bury the hatchet? You know, find a way to get along?"

Babs tapped a finger to her cheek. "Oh yes. It was rumored…well, I shouldn't talk about rumors." She leaned in. "It isn't nice to talk about people when they're not here."

"We already know about the affair rumor," Axel said.

"Oh?" Something glinted in Babs's eyes. Was it relief because now she could gossip since we already knew the dish? "Well in that case, you also probably know that it didn't end well."

Ha! I was right! She was happy to talk since we already knew the basics of the rumor.

"No, I didn't know it didn't end well." My voice struck an innocent tone. "They seemed to get along great at the competition. I mean, besides the fact that Saltz did sort of get on to Shelly when he thought she was working blood magic."

Babs pointed to the shelves and several books slid out and flew around the room before landing at the table before us.

"They don't get along well now at all," she confided. "They used to, but then I believe Shelly accused him of, well, using his position to oust her as potions mistress and taking her spot." She sighed dramatically. "Which of course forced Shelly to take on the task of teaching witch defense, which she didn't want to do. And of course in witch defense if you're going to teach defense, you have to have the children defend themselves against something, so…"

"So that's when the accusations of sorceress came into play," Axel said.

"Correct." Babs nodded. "If you want to show children the baddest of the bad and teach them how to fight against it, you have to do a bit of conjuring. So Shelly conjured a few entities, was deemed a sorceress and fired from the school for putting the lives of children in danger."

I hitched a brow. "Were they? Ever in danger?"

Babs lifted a shoulder. "Hard to say. I wasn't in the class, but I don't think Shelly ever would've hurt anyone. What I mean is, I don't believe she would've conjured something she couldn't control."

She inhaled deeply and smiled. "But what do I know? I'm simply a librarian."

Seemed Babs knew a lot. She could probably start her own celebrity gossip paper if she wanted.

She strolled to the books and sifted through them. "Let's see. I've pulled a few volumes on shifting." She leaned over to us. "We don't have many books on transmutation here, as you can imagine with the children around and all, but if you need one, I can unlock it from the basement. That's where we keep the big bad books." She giggled a touch manically at her own joke. I shivered.

"Aha!" Babs waved her hand, and a large, heavy, leather-bound book emerged from the stack. "Here's the Keating." She adjusted her glasses high on her nose and peeled back the cover. "Now then, let's see when this book was checked out last. No one ever asks for it, so I'm curious."

For all the magic in this place and Magnolia Cove, the checkout list was a pasted slip of paper on the back of the front cover. Babs scrolled her fingernail down the lines of names until she landed on the very last one.

"Ah, it was checked out over a year ago by one Gale East."

"Oh." I couldn't hide my surprise.

Babs whipped her glasses off. "Do you know her?"

My gaze flickered from her to Axel. "I do indeed. She almost killed my dragon."

NINE

"The girl who shot the potion ball at you? That's who checked out the Keating?"

Axel and I were in the Land Rover rumbling back toward the tunnel of love. Kidding. It wasn't a tunnel of love, but I could probably convince Axel to kiss me in the dark.

It wouldn't be too hard to make happen.

But not with Betty the Toad on my lap.

"Yes, Gale's the one who almost hit Hugo. Said she was working on a potion to help witches find magical creatures."

"He *is* magical," Axel murmured.

"But then I talked to her at the contest, too. She's the one who told me about Saltz and Shelly having an affair. She also mentioned she flunked out of the school."

Axel hitched a brow. "Flunked or was expelled?"

"Flunked."

"Hmmm." His lips coiled mysteriously.

"What?"

"Maybe she said flunked but was discharged for other reasons."

"And you think those reasons are that she was expelled and decided to lie about it instead and say she flunked."

"Of course." Axel winked. "Wouldn't you rather have flunked than been expelled?"

Was that a trick question? Neither option sounded like a winner. "Um...I would rather neither happen if you want to know the truth."

"That's because you're a responsible person."

I cackled. "You are so funny. Before I moved here, I was homeless, jobless and couldn't pay the bills. I wasn't a flunky in school, but I'd pretty much flunked life."

He took my hand and squeezed. Axel dragged his gaze from the road and studied me. "In case you haven't noticed, you've excelled here. In fact you've soared."

"Thanks for the pep talk."

"I mean it."

I brought his hand to my heart. "Seriously. Thank you." I glanced at Betty in the box of dirt. "But what are we about to do now?"

"Now, we're going to get creative." Axel took a right toward his house. "We've got some spellwork to do."

"WE'RE GOING to try to transmute Betty with our power."

I stood in Axel's cellar that was full of magical objects and talismans. The whole place seemed to buzz with power.

"You've been working some magic." I cocked a brow at him.

He nodded. "I've been doing what I've had to in order to figure out how best to help Betty."

"But you haven't figured it out yet."

He shook his head. "No, so I thought we'd try a combination of good old power and blood, sweat and tears."

"Seriously?"

"Seriously." He grabbed an ebony mortar from a shelf and placed it on a table. "The amount of blood it would normally take to work a transmutation spell is significant, so I thought if we combined both of ours, added some tears and sweat, then maybe we'll manage to knock her back into herself."

I pulled Keating's *Book of Spells* from my purse. "Do you think there are answers in here?"

He scowled. "Be careful with that."

"It's not like I'm going to start spouting incantations. I only wanted to scan through it, make sure the poppet spell is in there. Maybe there will be others that are useful."

His brows tightened to a severe line across his forehead. "Or dangerous."

"Or all of those," I said with sarcastic chipperness.

Axel growled.

I rolled my eyes. "I'll be careful."

He scowled. I smiled. The look of frustration melted from his face. Axel kissed my forehead. "Please do be careful because I really don't want to have to rescue you."

"When have you ever had to rescue me? Wait. Don't answer that. Can we please get on with this?"

Axel pulled his hair back and tied it. Then he took off his shirt and kicked off his shoes.

I almost dripped onto the floor. "Do you have to take your clothes off?"

"Control yourself." He smiled. "It makes it easier to feel the magic. You know that."

"Yes, I know. What are we doing?"

He pulled a knife from a sheath. I almost melted again, but this time from fear of blood instead of lust. "That looks horrifying."

"It's nothing compared to what the original spell calls for. I'm only doing a small cut on each of us and then tears."

I extended my hand. "If it will help Betty."

He took my hand. The warmth from his skin spread over my flesh. "No guarantees."

Axel slashed the knife over his thumb and then wrapped his hand. He did the same to me. It stung, but I needed my grand-mother back and a little bloodletting was nothing compared to helping her.

"Now for the tears." He inhaled. His chest heaved, and I had to strangle my urge to spread my fingers over his pecs. "Think of something sad."

We stared at each other and burst out laughing. "Stop," I demanded. "Don't stare at me. It's doing the wrong thing. I'm supposed to be sad."

"Okay, I'll stop."

I stared at the table until I felt the tears surface. It wasn't hard. All I had to do was concentrate on what it would feel like to lose Betty, a woman I was only just beginning to know.

Seconds later tears were spilling. I was so good at it I felt like creating a new profession—professional crier. I could make millions, but only if people wanted to buy my tears.

Probably no one would ever want to do that. Scratch my plan to achieve millions.

The mortar appeared under my chin and my tears dripped into the bowl.

I hadn't seen Axel cry, but I knew he had. He wiped a hand over his face and inhaled deeply.

"Now for the words."

He opened his hands, and a book on a pedestal unfurled. The pages flipped for several seconds and then stopped with a flourish. Axel chanted quietly, and I immediately noticed a shift in the air.

It felt like the barometric pressure dropped. That's the only way I can describe it. Like an unseen cloud had dropped from heaven and was pushing down on the room. The energy had completed shifted. I only prayed what Axel was doing worked.

Betty remained unchanged. She sat on top of the dirt; her throat expanding and contracting as she did whatever it is toads do.

Axel's voice rose. He dipped his hand in a pouch and tossed a silvery powder into the mortar. The blood and tears flamed. Axel dropped his hand in the flames, plucked out a fiery ball of goo and dropped it on Betty. The toad didn't flinch.

Axel stopped chanting, and we both waited.

The toad didn't change. Not good. I shot Axel a hopeful look. "Is there more? Maybe?"

His shoulders sagged. "No. It was the best shot we had without making a sacrifice."

"Ew. I'm not making a sacrifice."

"Me neither. But that's how it used to be done."

I ran a finger along Betty's back. "Don't worry. We'll figure out a way to help you. We won't let you be stuck like this forever."

I sank onto a chair and watched as Axel tugged his shirt back on. "What about the bands? Do you think those will work?"

Axel slumped onto a chair. "From what I've read, the amount of power it would take might disappoint you."

I hooked my legs under me. "What do you mean? How would I be disappointed?"

He folded his arms. "Here's the thing about those bands. I already explained they work the best when both beings can talk. Since you can't reach Betty and your entire plan is to reach her, by using the bands, you'll wipe out all the magic in them in one try."

I pressed at a worry line forming between my brows. "I'll wipe out their magic? You mean they won't work?"

He shook his head. "No. They'll work fine. I think. But they'll work too good. The bands will reach out to link the two of you, but you'll be using them in a way that they weren't intended. You'll use up all their magic."

"So I won't be able to use them on you."

He nodded.

My heart sank. The bands would break? By using them on Betty, I would basically be destroying their power.

So I wouldn't have them for what I wanted—which was to help Axel.

What was more important? Freeing my grandmother from her prison or helping Axel? I mean, Axel had survived this long without my help. Why did I seem to think I had to change him?

I guess that's just who I was. And besides, when I first met Axel, he was tortured by the wolf. He didn't even want to date me. He carried his burden like a curse. I didn't want him to feel that way.

I loved him and wanted him to shine like the star he was.

Yes, I know it was cheesy, but that's how I felt.

I exhaled and untucked my legs. "If that's what it takes, then that's what it takes. I'll use the bands on Betty. I doubt I'll have another choice."

He raked his fingers over his chest. Axel crossed to me. He wrapped his hands around my waist and pulled me to my feet.

"I know you want those cuffs for me. We'll keep looking. There will be other choices. Don't worry. I'll keep searching. There has to be another way."

"I don't know." I felt my knees weaken.

He heaved me up. "Don't do that. Don't give up. That's not the Pepper Dunn I know. You keep trying to reach Betty. There may be another reason why you can't talk to her and it just needs to be unlocked."

"But how do I do that?" I said.

His smile warmed me to my toes. "You have an entire shopful of creatures. Sometimes animals can reach other animals even if they can't reach people. Try that. See if the other creatures at Familiar Place can talk to her. Maybe they'll discover something you can't."

I leaned my head on Axel's chest. "Okay. I'll do it. But what about Shelly's things?"

"What do you mean?"

I leaned back. "She showed Betty how to make the potion. Where would she have done that?"

"Her house." Axel rocked back on his heels. "Wherever she was staying in town. Of course. I'll see what I can find out about her ingredients. See if I can recreate it."

"Axel, she had to have written down or saved the potion somewhere. You know how it is. I mean, I realized that when I was tinkering with my own potion—you have to record every detail, every change you make. Otherwise you'll never remember what you were doing."

"She doesn't work at the school anymore so she wouldn't have an office there."

"But she might have one at her house. It's at least worth trying to find out."

He kissed the top of my head. "You're a genius. I don't know why I didn't think of that before. I'll see if Bo can help with that. And in the meantime you should see if you can communicate with Betty."

I frowned. "I know what I need to do, but there's more than that."

"Oh?"

"I'm going to check the Keating. I've got the book. I want to make sure the poppet spell is in there."

He pressed his forehead to mine. The clean scent of his hair wafted up my nostrils. "Don't work the spell."

I rolled my eyes. "I wasn't planning on it. I only want to look and understand it. Plus, you and I both smelled the sulfur scent. I want to take a look at the spell and see what I can learn from it."

"Like?"

"Like how far away you have to be to have a poppet. What you need to have from the person to create one. Things that could help us."

Axel smirked. "I know one thing that will definitely help us."

"What's that?"

"Tracking down Gale East and finding out what she knows about poppets."

I smiled. "I think you're right. But where am I going to find her?"

"Oh, Pepper," he teased, "don't you know that when witches don't get to show off their New Year's potions for the contest, they're very unhappy."

A bubble of hope ballooned in my chest. "They are?"

"Yes. Witches make sure they can one-up each other. They'll want to prove how smart and talented and overall superior they are."

I laughed. "So where will I find them?"

His luscious lips spread into a smile that reminded me of sunshine. "Easy. At the witch coffeehouse getting nice and warm, drinking coffee and showing off their potions."

TEN

*B*efore I could throw myself into the line of potion makers at the coffeehouse, I first had not only to grab my own potion but to also read up on poppets.

All I knew was that crap better not take too long because I had Betty to save, for goodness' sake. Whoever killed Shelly had the potion that could save Betty.

Sorry, not *could,* would. It would absolutely save Betty and I needed that to happen. Like yesterday.

I raced back to the house on my cast-iron skillet. Betty was tucked snugly under my arm. Note to self—get her back in water ASAP. Toads and frogs needed water, right? They had to keep their skin moist or else they'd dry out and die.

Ever seen a dried-up, dead frog? I have and it's not cute.

Anyway, I reached the house and headed inside only to find my cousins in a full-blown argument.

"How dare you invite him here and put me to sleep!" Cordelia slammed her fist on the table.

Amelia shrugged as if drugging her cousin was no big deal. "It was only herbal tea. Besides, you were asleep. You didn't care who was here."

Cordelia's face crimsoned to such a dark shade I thought her head might pop off and rocket into space. "That's not the point! How many times do I have to say it? They don't care about us. I don't know why our dads are here now, but they left us back then. They want something, Amelia. Can't you see that?"

Amelia's face crumpled. I wanted to reach out and wrap her in my arms. Thing is, Cordelia was wrong. Their dads hadn't been in their lives because Mint and Licky had forbidden it.

But I wasn't supposed to know that.

So what could I do? What could I say that might smooth things over? There were only a few options. One, I might tell them that Mint and Licky had left their fathers, but that would create an entirely new bowl of problems like, why did I know that? As well as a litany of other accusations I wasn't particularly interested in sifting through.

Two, I could simply say that Cordelia needed to calm down. Explain that I was sure their dads wanted to be a part of their lives for a good reason. Cordelia would ask how I knew that, and I would explain it was a witch sense sort of like Spiderman's spidey sense. Cordelia would respond by punching me in the face.

So two was definitely out. Three, I could just tell my cousins what their fathers were—genies—and let them accuse me of keeping secrets. Once again I was back to keeping knowledge from my two best friends on earth.

It really ticked me off that my aunts had placed me in such a stupid position. Whichever way it turned out, when my cousins realized I knew stuff about them that even they didn't know, let alone suspect, there would be fiery heck to pay.

The question was—did I want to pay sooner or later?

Was it best to rip off the Band-Aid or slowly peel it back?

I was always one for ripping—best to get the pain over quickly.

As my cousins bickered with one another, I readied myself. Had to get the words just right. Had to mix and max so that it worked the way it needed to and if something was going to happen, it would happen the exact way it should.

Wishes were a funny thing. I mean, I didn't know that for sure, but it seemed a pretty good guess.

Though Mint and Licky hadn't given me any specifics on wish making, I knew that if one of them had started a sentence with "I wish," then one of their husbands granted it. Unfortunately it hadn't been granted the way the sentence had been spoken. But that was a risk I was willing to take.

Amelia and Cordelia had been around their fathers a few times, and they were worked up. Like, seriously worked up. They were wound to the point that I knew I'd be able to have an impact.

I inhaled a deep breath and said very loudly, "I wish I had black hair."

My cousins stopped arguing and slowly turned their heads to me. Betty the Toad stared at me as well. She knew the secret—that Cordelia and Amelia's fathers were half genie. She knew it, but Mint and Licky didn't know she knew.

Say that three times fast.

"What did you say?" Amelia cocked her head at me.

"I said"—I cleared my throat and spoke as clear as I could—"I wish I had black hair."

"Why would you wish for that?" She frowned. "Your hair is so pretty."

"Yeah, at least be blonde like the two of us." Cordelia raked her fingers through her hair. "Everyone knows blondes have more fun."

"I was only wishing for it." I deflated. It didn't work. I never should even have tried.

"But why would you wish for it when you can just do it?" Amelia's face squinched in confusion. "You're a witch. A head witch at that."

"Oh, I don't know." I stroked Betty's head and glared back at her. Good thing the toad couldn't speak. She'd probably be telling them why I blurted out such a stupid sentence. "I just thought maybe I could wish for something, and you know, it would stop the two of you from arguing about your dads. Your dads are witches, right? What sort of witches are they?"

Cordelia scoffed. "Heck if I know or care. They're stupid witches.

Selfish witches. Annoying witches that I don't want to have anything to do with."

"Stop it." Amelia's expression darkened. "Stop it right there. Our dads are good people. They are kind, and so what? They made a mistake. I know you like to think you're Miss Perfect, Cordelia. But you're not."

Then it happened. The simple fact that the two of them were talking about their dads caused something to change in the air. Magic whirled around Amelia's hands. It looked like shooting stars streaking around her fingers. Or like a whirling tornado of gossamer.

It was freaking cool.

Amelia noticed and raised her palms. "What's going on?"

"I wish I had black hair."

Amelia's eyes flared. Panic splashed across her face. Her lips trembled. "I don't know why, but I feel an urge to help you, Pepper. It's so stupid. But I feel the urge to grant your wish."

She raised one of her hands. Power danced over her flesh. She pointed the finger at me. My scalp tingled, and I knew it was happening. I knew Amelia was granting my wish.

"Am I supposed to be impressed by this?" Cordelia flipped a long strand of hair over one shoulder. "It's simple magic."

The tingle washed down my scalp to my back. The magic surrounding Amelia faded, and she stared at her hands and then at me.

"That was so weird." She clutched her chest. "I didn't work magic. It didn't feel like it. I felt, I don't know—compelled to grant your wish."

Cordelia glanced at me and laughed. "Only you didn't do it right."

"Why not?" I said.

"Look in the mirror," Cordelia said.

Amelia's fingers flew to her mouth. "Oh no. Pepper. I'm so sorry. I don't know what happened."

"It can't be that bad." My stomach roiled as if a gallon of worms were rooting in it. Of course it *could* be that bad. I'd remembered what Mint and Licky had told me about their husband's wishing ability.

Around them, wish granting had gone sour and become chaotic, for lack of a better description.

I glanced in a mirror. My jaw dropped. My hair was white. Pure white. Not black. Not chic. Not platinum. But old-lady white. It was horrible.

"I can change it back." Amelia's voice rose three octaves. She took my hands. "I know I can."

I tamped down the panic fighting to clamber up my throat. "It'll be okay. I know you can fix it. No problem." I smiled widely. "It's as simple as me saying, I wish I had red hair. My hair. I wish I had my hair color back."

"Oh my gosh, I feel that weird thing stirring in me." Amelia flapped her hands. "It's coming."

"Probably a stomach bug," Cordelia said in a bored tone. But she didn't look bored. She watched the entire spectacle like a hawk on the hunt.

Magic poured from Amelia's hands. I felt the tingle again. When it was finished, I glanced at Amelia, who grimaced.

My hopes plummeted to the floor. "It's not better, is it?"

"It's black," Amelia croaked.

"Well at least that's the original color she wanted," Cordelia said. "Step aside and let me handle this."

She shoved Amelia away and cracked her knuckles. She wiggled her fingers, but I didn't feel a tingle of any sort.

"It didn't work," Amelia said flatly. "You didn't fix her, Cordelia. It's worse."

Oh God. How could it be worse? Was it green? I glanced in the mirror. Back to white. It was back to old-lady white.

Cordelia glanced at her hands. "I don't understand. It should have worked. I've never had a problem with my magic before. I've even reversed spells that you've done, Amelia. I've been able to make it happen in the past. Why didn't it work now?"

I had a very bad feeling that this was part of the wishing magic. Unfortunately I wasn't the person to explain it to them even though I knew the secret.

Cordelia's gaze slowly dragged from her hands to me. "You know something, don't you, Pepper?"

I scoffed. "I have no idea what you're talking about."

Amelia pointed at me. "You do. You made a wish, and then you made it again. Why did you do that? Why didn't you just work the magic yourself? And why is my magic broken? I don't understand."

I sighed. "Look. I'm not the best person to explain this to you."

"Explain what?" Cordelia folded her arms. "*What* aren't you the best person to explain to us?"

I cringed and tucked a strand of bright white hair behind one ear. "Well, you see—"

"What she's trying to say is that you girls have special powers."

The three of us whirled around. The front door was open and standing there were Bean, Amelia's father, Morgan, Cordelia's dad, and Mint and Licky.

"We should've told you girls a long time ago," Mint whispered.

"But the timing never seemed right," Licky added.

"We're sorry." Mint wove her fingers through her hair.

Licky smiled. "But now we can tell you."

"Tell us what?" Cordelia fisted her hands. "If someone doesn't start talking soon, I'm going to disown all of you."

Amelia looked impressed. "Wow. That's a lot of people."

"The holidays will be quieter," Cordelia said. "No cooked turkeys running around the dining room."

Amelia snorted. "You'd miss it."

Cordelia hitched a shoulder. "I doubt it." She pinned her attention back on the gang in the doorway. "What is it? What is it y'all have to tell us?"

Morgan, an extremely tall and fit bald man, stepped forward. "My dears, what we have to tell y'all is that you're special."

Cordelia rolled her eyes. "There's got to be more to it than that. This is America. Everyone is special here."

"But you are more special," Morgan said. "Your blood holds very special genes."

Cordelia crossed her arms. "What kind of special genes?"

Morgan smiled. "My beloved, in your veins dwells the blood of the ancients. You are witches, but you are more than that. You are wish granters—genies. You have the ability to bestow wishes on people."

Amelia and Cordelia exchanged a long glance. Finally Amelia looked back at the throng of people. "I always knew I was special." She pointed at me. "Now tell me how to fix her hair."

ELEVEN

While my cousins and their parents had a quiet chat in the living room about being part genie and what that meant, I grabbed Betty and headed into the kitchen to peruse the Keating.

Hugo played outside in the backyard. Mattie was curled up on a floor-heating vent.

"Warmest place in town," she said through a yawn. "What in the world happened to your hair?"

I tugged on a strand. "Oh. A wish gone wrong."

"Looks like that wish went more than wrong. That wish turned sour on you and died."

"Thank you. That makes me feel better."

The cat blinked. "I'm sorry. I'll try to be more sensitive. What you got there, sugarbear?"

"This? Oh, it's Keating's *Book of Spells.*"

"Gives me the willies just thinking about it." Mattie stretched and jumped on the table. "Why in all the great big world do you have that book?"

"Well, I need to learn about poppets."

"Page three hundred and six."

I blinked. "What?"

"I know the Keating. Your mother had a copy."

I nearly fell to the floor. "You're kidding?"

"I am not."

I peeled back the cover and glanced at the table of contents. "But there are spells in here for summoning demons, creating love potions, conjuring the dead."

"Your mother went through a period of experimentation in her teenage years."

That made sense. I shrugged. "Most kids do, I guess. But Betty let her read this?"

"Of course not," Mattie snapped. "Your mother snuck it in like contraband."

"Wow. Did she ever make a poppet?"

"No."

I stared at Mattie. She blinked slowly and proceeded to lick a paw and wash her face.

"You answered too quickly. So my mom made a poppet."

"Maybe."

I sighed and raked my fingers through my hair. "Listen, I'm not judging. I'm only trying to make sure Shelly Seay was killed by the use of one. That's all. And maybe how far away they'd need to be in order to effectively use a poppet."

"Three hundred and six," Mattie repeated. "That's the page which will explain everything you need to know."

I flipped through the book. The yellowed pages were brittle and disintegrating at the ends. As I turned, I was careful not to tear any of the sheets.

"Here we are, page three hundred and six. *The use of poppets.*" I scanned the page. "Says here poppets can be made of many things—clay, cloth, even aluminum foil if you need quick protection."

"Hmmm. Keep reading."

"This just gives a list of ingredients for basic spells—protection, how to stop a gossip, money. It doesn't say how to use a poppet to kill someone."

"Turn the page," Mattie instructed.

Hugo scratched at the back door. I rose and let him inside. Then I returned to my seat. The dragon slumped to the floor in front of me, and I propped my legs on him.

"Oh wow. It's right here. *How to use poppets to destroy your enemies.* You weren't kidding. Okay. Let me see the ingredients. A feather from a black crow, a buzzard's beak—ew. This is gross."

"Only a fool reads the Keating to put themselves in a good mood."

I glared at Mattie. "I'm reading to understand what happened. At the potion contest, Axel and I smelled sulfur. It was strong and gross. Horrible. I don't see anything in here that could've smelled like that."

"Then you haven't reached the last ingredient."

"Let's see-dragon's breath. Wait." My mind whirled. "Dragon's breath? That's a weird ingredient."

"You're trying to kill someone, not make a peach cobbler."

"I guess that's true." I scanned the list until I found what she meant. "Rotten eggs—which would smell like sulfur."

"Ain't you smart?"

I tapped my fingers on the page. "So that would've been the sulfur we smelled. But I've got to find the poppet. It isn't enough that we think one was used. I need to know more."

I nibbled my bottom lip as I remembered something Axel had said. "Mattie?"

"Yes, sugar?"

"Do you think you could talk to Betty? I can't talk to her. I'm not sure why. Axel thought maybe another animal would be able to reach her."

"I can try."

The cat slinked over to Betty and touched noses with the toad. Betty didn't move. After several seconds Mattie broke away.

"Girl, we've got a problem."

That didn't sound good. "What do you mean, we've got a problem? That's Betty in there."

Mattie padded to the other side of the table and stared at the toad.

"I cain't get through to her. I don't know what it is. I'm not sure if it's the frog brain—"

"Toad. She's a toad," I clarified.

"That's what I said. I ain't sure if it's her toad brain or what, but I cain't hear one lick of sound coming through that there brain of hers. Usually I can hear something. Or sense something, but there ain't nothin' there for me to sense."

I did my best to ease the rising panic in my chest. This was bad. No, this wasn't bad. This could be horrible.

Wait. Maybe I needed to take a few breaths and get a grip. Yes. I needed a grip. To calm down.

"But surely that doesn't mean anything," I said. "Surely you can't hear her just because she's a toad and you're not an amphibian."

"You're not a cat, but you can talk to me."

I scoffed. "Everyone can talk to you because you're a talking cat."

Mattie rubbed her whiskers. "What I'm saying is that I think it's more than simply the fact that Betty's a toad that's the problem."

"Okay. So what is it?"

I did everything I could to shove down the dread rising in my throat. It didn't work. My chest flushed from nerves.

"I think that Betty the toad is a problem because she's forgetting who she is."

I grimaced. "You think she isn't communicating because she doesn't remember she's Betty?"

"Right," Mattie said, "and if we don't save her soon, we'll lose her forever."

TWELVE

That was all I needed to hear. Betty had to be freed ASAP. I had called Axel, but there wasn't an answer. I would be forced to use the bands I'd bought him and myself for Christmas. There was no doubt about it. But since I couldn't reach him, maybe there was something else I could do that would at least help us along.

I rushed from the kitchen with Hugo at my heels and ran smack into my cousins and aunts and I guess uncles, even though we weren't blood related.

"Pepper," Amelia said, "do you want me to fix your hair?"

Morgan squeezed Amelia's hand. "We've discussed this already. It's not how wishes work."

Crap. If I had a horrible feeling about Betty, I had an almost-horrible feeling about my cousins as one-quarter genies. A feeling, I would like to add, that I had brought upon myself when I wished for hair of another color.

Stupid me. Seriously. I should've known better.

I shoved my hands in my coat sleeves. "Don't worry about it right now, Amelia. We can discuss it when I get back. But Betty and Mattie are in the kitchen. Can y'all look after them?"

"We'd love to," Cordelia said. I looked for a glimmer of sarcasm in her words, but she smiled widely. "Seriously. We'd love to watch them. Go on."

I grabbed my cast-iron skillet and nudged Hugo out the door. "Come on, boy, let's go have a chocolate mocha."

GARGOYLE'S GRIND was located on Bubbling Cauldron, along the main strip. It was a cozy little joint that featured live music, open mic nights and even open witchcraft nights for witches interested in testing a new spell on folks and for folks who enjoyed watching and learning new spells.

It also happened, on this day, to be the home of the potion contestant support group. Where witches who'd wanted to dazzle the world with their latest potion had witnessed their dreams die in flames when Shelly Seay was murdered.

And I was about to join them.

It only took a few moments to spot the circle of witches. They took up one side of the shop, having pushed several four-tops together to make one gigantic table.

I ordered a coffee for me and bought a dog biscuit for Hugo. Yes, he likes fresh meat better, but he would take a doggie treat, especially one covered in icing, anytime he could.

I led him to the back of the table, where there happened to be one open spot.

The young man, Anthony, the one who had led Saltz Swift away to start the judging, was speaking.

"I didn't make a potion this year. I wished I had, but I wanted to be the stage manager of the show. So I commend all of you for making potions. There have been some great ones. Some I'd never heard of, and also others I wished I was smart enough to have come up with."

His head of curls bobbed as he nodded toward Gale East. "Tell us what you brought, Gale."

Gale's gaze dropped to her hands folded in her lap. "It's nothing, really."

"It's definitely something," Anthony prodded her gently. "It's an achievement to even enter the contest."

"I don't know."

Anthony pushed up his sleeves. "Do you realize how many people say they're going to enter the contest but don't?"

Gale lifted her eyes shyly. "How many?"

"Hundreds. Thousands." Anthony might've been reaching with the *thousands* comment, but hey, who was I to judge?

Gale slowly smiled. "Yeah?"

"Yeah." You could almost see Anthony's gusto. "Absolutely. So tell us what you made."

Gale rubbed her face like she was trying to smooth out wrinkles, and smiled. "I created a potion that will help anyone find a magical creature."

A few oohs and ahhhs drifted from the table.

She cleared her throat. "How many times have you been in the middle of an important spell and realized you didn't have a feather from a griffin? Or fur from a talking bunny?"

Lots of murmurs of "me" and "and the time" popped up.

Gale tapped a fist on the table. "Me too. So many."

Who were these witches that they didn't read the spells before they started them? That was like making a recipe before reading the whole thing.

Oh wait. I'm sure I've done that before and realized I was missing something or needed something.

Okay, so maybe Gale Wind—I mean, East—had a point.

She pulled a porcelain bottle from her purse. "So I wanted to make it easy and help witches find these creatures. I wanted to take the guesswork out of creature searching."

A lady with wiry gray hair clapped. "Bravo!"

Gale's gaze cut to Hugo, who lay stretched on the floor, happily gobbling his dog treat. She glanced at me. Her eyes flared. Oh, the hair. Right. I still had old-lady white hair. I shrugged and smiled.

"May I demonstrate on your dragon?" Gale nodded to Hugo.

I waved my hand. "Go right ahead."

She opened the porcelain box. I couldn't see the liquid from where I sat, but Gale pulled a cotton ball from her pocket.

She concentrated on pouring the bluish potion onto the cotton. "I've tried lots of things, but cotton works the best. You could maybe try an old T-shirt if you had to. That might work too."

The ball rose from her hand. It was now a golden color and reminded me of a tiny sun. I wondered if it had its own heat.

Gale spoke directly to the orb. "Find me a dragon, for it is a dragon I seek. It must breathe fire and have scales from head to toe for the spell I need."

The ball whizzed to the ceiling like a gunshot. It darted left and right before coming to a quick stop. It spun around, then dropped with amazing speed back to Gale.

"Go," she said, "I will follow."

Then the orb sailed over to Hugo and hovered over his head. Hugo snapped at the orb as if biting at annoying flies.

Gale's mouth split into a wide grin. "That's it. That's how it's done."

The table erupted into applause. Even I clapped. That had been pretty impressive.

She opened her palm, and the cotton ball zipped to her and sank into her cupped hand. Gale crushed the ball and looked up at all of us proudly. "Thank you. Thank all of y'all."

Anthony's gaze flickered to me. "A new guest snuck into our midst. Please, introduce yourself."

Oh Lord. All eyes were on me. Adrenaline rocketed through my body. I hated speaking in front of folks. It was the worst. But I had no choice. Betty must be saved.

"Umm hmmm. I'm Pepper Dunn. I don't normally look like this. I usually have red hair. I'm way too young to have a few grays let alone a full head of them. Let's call it a wish gone wrong."

Several silver-haired witches glared at me.

"Sorry. Anyway, I'm here because of my grandmother. Many of you may know her. Betty Craple."

A few murmurs of recognition rose from the table.

"Yes, well, she was turned into a toad by Shelly Seay, and now she's trapped."

A knot filled my chest. It bore down on me, suffocating, cutting off my air and filling me with pain.

It was horrible. I always thought things would work out. That everything would be fine, but what if it wasn't? What if Axel and I couldn't find a solution? What if Betty was stuck as a toad forever? What if Shelly's potion was never discovered and no one was pinned for her murder?

I knuckled away several tears. "Anyway, I'm here not because I have a potion to share. I did make one but...I don't know what I'm doing anymore. I'm here because I need your help. Shelly Seay was murdered. I know she was, and unless we can discover who killed her, my grandmother will remain a toad forever."

I received a few sympathetic smiles, but that was it. Anthony waited a few seconds.

"If anyone knows something that will help Pepper, please be sure to tell her." He crossed his arms on the table and tapped his fingers. "Now, who's next?"

When the meeting finished up, I approached Gale. It was way too coincidental that her potion had originally targeted Hugo and then the poppet spell had needed dragon's breath.

Was it possible that she'd been able to snag some of Hugo's breath when the potion went after him?

She'd just shouldered her purse when I shot her a wide smile. As I sidled up, I realized I'd forgotten how small Gale was. Maybe only five feet tall or so with messy dark hair that just brushed her chin.

"Hey, Gale. That was so cool. Love your potion."

She laughed nervously. "Yeah, well, it turned out a lot better than the other day, didn't it? I hope I didn't scare you then."

"No, not at all." Hugo bounded up beside me, and I patted his head. "But it's so funny about that. I was looking at an old spell book the other day and came across one that needed dragon's breath. If I didn't already have one—a dragon, I mean—I'd have a hard time finding some."

Gale puffed out her chest with pride. "Which is why you'd need my spell."

"Yeah." My gaze drifted away. "You know the spell book was a really interesting one. What was the name of it?" I tapped a finger to my chin. "I remember!" I snapped my fingers. "It was Keating's something or other—*Book of Spells,* I think. Ever heard of it?"

Her eyes flared. Of course she'd heard of it. Gale had checked it out.

She recovered by tucking a stubby strand of hair behind her ear. "Nope. No. I've never heard of it. Sounds like an interesting book."

"It is," I mused. "Very interesting. Lots of unique spells."

Her gaze darted to her watch. "Oh, well. Look at that. I have to get going."

I grabbed Hugo's leash. "See you around."

I watched her walk off and didn't hear the person padding up behind me until I felt something brush over my shoulders.

I jerked back. Anthony smiled. "You had some hair on you. Just getting it off."

"Thanks." I wasn't sure at all if I was grateful or creeped out. What guy brushed loose strands of hair from a stranger's shoulders?

But my uncertainty was quickly replaced when he nodded toward Gale. "Interesting potion."

"It was." I put as much cheer into my voice as possible.

"Listen." Anthony's speech lowered. He fingered his glasses up his nose and glanced side to side. "That Gale. I don't want to tell you anything that may worry you, but she's strange."

"How do you mean?"

"She was always working spells that were kind of dark, sinister."

I pointed to Hugo. "You mean the sort of craft that would involve him?"

"Among other beings." He shivered. "I don't want to make you nervous or say she's guilty of anything, but when she was at the school of magic, Gale dabbled in dark stuff. Really dark stuff. Shelly Seay was her mentor."

That took me by surprise. "Her mentor?"

The knot in Anthony's throat bobbed when he swallowed. "They were really close."

"How do you know all this?"

"Oh, well I work at the school." He raked his fingers through his hair. "I'm not anybody special. I do a lot of the class scheduling. No one pays much attention to me, so I have time to pay attention to them."

I studied his soft, round face that reminded me of dough, his bright eyes that were sharp yet kind. Anthony seemed absolutely harmless.

I leaned in. "What else can you tell me about Gale?"

He cleared his throat. "I can tell you it was because she worked a spell full of dark magic that she was expelled from school."

"What sort of spell?"

He licked his full lips. "A poppet spell."

THIRTEEN

"What happened to your hair?"

"Do we have to discuss it?"

Axel and I sat at Spellin' Skillet grabbing a quick bite to eat as we regrouped.

He pointed to my white tendrils. "I like it."

I nearly raked my fingers down my face. I mean, was he kidding? "You're only saying that."

"No, I'm not. It's like stardust."

"I look a thousand years old."

"Only to an old man."

I choked on a sip of sweet tea. "That might be the almost nicest compliment I've ever received in my life."

He winked. "You're welcome." Axel cut into a country-fried steak. "So how'd the hair happen?"

"My cousins are officially genies. Well, part genies." I scooped a forkful of creamed corn and popped it in my mouth. Oh, sheer bliss. Corn and cream and butter. Seriously, there was absolutely nothing wrong with this combination.

"How do you manage to eat fried foods and stay so fit?" I said.

"I run. I'm also part werewolf." He waved his fork. "That helps."

"Aren't you lucky."

He hitched a dark and luscious brow. "I guess I am. Now, did your cousins figure out the genie thing on their own?"

"You just have to pry, don't you?"

"Love, I know when you've had something to do with things."

I shuddered. The word *love* on his tongue made my body turn to jelly. "They were arguing, and well, I guess I kind of forced it."

"Kind of?"

Heat flushed my cheeks. "They were going to kill each other over their dads. Do we trust them? Do we not? Well, I made a wish and Amelia granted it."

"Very badly." He sliced into an asparagus spear. "Problem is, I think only the genie who granted the wish can fix it."

I groaned. "Then I have no chance of ever getting my original hair back."

He grabbed my hand. I fissure of fire blazed over my flesh. Our gazes snapped like locks into place.

"I will make sure you're taken care of," Axel murmured. "If I haven't made that clear before, you should know. That is my duty in life."

"You're only duty?"

"Let's not push things." He laughed. "Yes, it's my main duty. Keeping you safe and protected."

"Along with fighting crime, of course."

Mischief sparked in his eyes. "Of course."

We hadn't said the word *love* that much since we'd confessed it and Axel had then vanished without a trace for weeks, but I knew he loved me.

Before I could focus on that too much, however, Axel brought me back to the now. "So, did you recite poetry at Gargoyle's Grind?"

"How'd you know?" I laughed. "No. But I did discover that Gale East—"

"The one who checked out Keating?"

"Yes. She was expelled from the school for the use of poppets. So you were right. She didn't flunk out after all."

Axel rose. He whipped on his jacket. I followed suit.

"What're you doing?"

He tossed back the last bit of coffee in his mug. "Isn't it obvious? We're going to have a little conversation with Gale East."

I shouldered my purse as my phone buzzed. I slid it from my pocket. "Hello?"

"Pepper." Cordelia's voice rose in panic.

"What's wrong?" I tried not to let her panic overcome me. I gritted my teeth and tightened my neck. I knew it had to do with Betty. It just had to.

"Betty looks sick."

"How sick?"

Axel shot me a questioning look, and I mouthed, *Betty.* He folded his arms. The expression of worry on his face made me feel worse.

"She's turning pale. I don't know what's wrong, but you'd better come home."

I thumbed off the phone. Axel pulled me to him and pressed his lips to my head. "Betty?"

I curled my fingers into his jacket and inhaled his scent. "She's not okay. I think she might be sick." Tears filled my eyes. "Axel," I whimpered.

He gripped my hand in a vice of comfort and strength. "Let's go."

WE REACHED the house a few minutes later. Mint and Licky were there along with Cordelia and Amelia.

"What's wrong with her?" I said.

Mint ran a finger down Betty's head. "She looks bad. When did she last eat?"

"I took her to the shop. Gosh, when was that? My days are all confused. I think it was this morning. She ate about a thousand crickets."

Axel closed his eyes and sighed. "Has she gone to the bathroom yet?"

I shook my head. "No."

"Probably just constipation."

Mint, Licky, Cordelia and Amelia stared at Axel. I tucked a strand of white hair behind my ear. "I'm sorry?"

Axel pressed a hand to Betty's sides. "Constipation can cause you to feel sick. If it can do that to humans, it will do the same to animals."

Amelia chewed her fingernail. "Hmm. Amphibian constipation. Who would've thought it?"

I dropped my purse to the floor. "Not me."

Axel handed Betty to me, and when I felt her sides, I knew it was true. "Her stomach is tight, y'all."

Axel winked. "Looks like you better rub it."

I laid Betty on her back. She fought a little, but once I started rubbing her belly, she settled down. After about ten minutes I felt her stomach rumble. I set her in her box, and next thing you knew, she had emptied out her plumbing.

So to speak.

I was sweating, y'all—sweating when we arrived. Nerves, I guess. Betty was so fragile it was pointless to wait until we found the potion. We had to do something, and we needed to do it now.

As if he was reading my mind, Axel pulled the magical cuffs from his jacket. "You ready to try these?"

I pushed my bravest smile to my face. "Let me grab my pair."

I dug my matching cuffs from my bedroom, where I found Mattie stretched on my bed.

"You gonna try to reach Betty, sugar?"

"What choice do I have?"

"No choice, I guess. You need some moral support?"

I sank to the bed and threaded my fingers through my hair. "Yes. I need a ton of moral support. It's so stupid. These cuffs were for Axel and I don't mind using them on Betty but I just always feel that every chance I have with Axel to connect with his wolf—there's always something in the way."

"Makes it better, don't you think?" Mattie rubbed her face against my bicep. "When it all works out, I mean."

"Yeah." The frustration I felt was stupid. Inside me was a bottomless well of love for Betty. There would always be cuffs. There would always be a way to reach Axel.

I exhaled a shot of air. "Sometimes when you hold on to something too tightly, it makes it harder to stay, or work."

"That is so true, girl." Mattie sat and blinked. "I know when I've tried to keep some Tom around, the more I force it, the worse it is."

I nodded. "Sometimes you just gotta let life click into place without pushing too much."

"I would say so." Mattie nudged the cuffs. "Now. Are you gonna try to reach Betty so we can learn how to make the potion?"

I pushed off the bed. Renewed energy coursed through my veins. "Yeah. Yeah, I am. Thanks, Mattie. I needed to be reminded that sometimes it's better to give to someone else than it is to force something that might not be."

"Everything will work on in the end, sugarbear." Mattie jumped off the bed and padded toward the door. "It always does."

When my foot hit the very last stair was when I noticed the house was dark except for about a million candles. Most of them sat on surfaces, but some of them floated.

Floated!

My stomach tightened. I really wished this had been a date night with Axel and not a moment when I was trying to save Betty.

Note to self—remind Axel to light floating candles the next time we were alone in his house.

Of course if there were floating candles, there might end up being other things that floated. Namely me, to a land of ecstasy. It would be the first time but hopefully not the last.

But those thoughts were my own and not to be shared.

My gaze snagged on Axel's. His eyes were dark and full of something that made my chest constrict.

I felt like he was thinking the exact thing as me. My gaze darted away as I tucked a strand of stupid white hair behind my ear.

Way to look sexy, Pepper. Thanks, Amelia, for giving me white hair.

It was all my fault. I knew it.

Mint and Licky had apparently left, leaving Cordelia, Amelia and Axel. I quirked a brow at Axel.

"We thought it best not to have chaos witches here while we work this spell."

"Yeah, as if broken part-genies aren't bad enough," Amelia said.

I wanted to wrap my arms around her shoulders and give her a good solid squeeze. There was nothing worse than beating yourself up for something you couldn't help.

"It's not your fault my hair's white."

"We can try to fix it. After. My dad gave me some tips."

Cordelia snickered. "Just don't turn it green."

"Why would you even say that?" Amelia brought her fists to her face. "Suggesting it makes it even worse. It puts it in my mind. That is so annoying."

Cordelia flipped her hair over one shoulder. "That's what you get for hanging out with our dads."

"I thought you were getting over your anger, Cordelia."

She turned her gaze to me. "It's gone from red-hot rage to simmering distaste."

"Give it time. Sometimes the best relationships start out rocky." My gaze slipped to Axel. A knowing smile graced his lips. A rush of heat flamed on my neck. I glanced away.

"Let's get started."

I slid the cuffs over my wrists. This was a good look. Sort of medieval warrior woman. I liked it. I could be the next She-Ra, Princess of Power. I could definitely dig it, y'all.

I nodded to Axel. "You have your cuffs?"

He pulled them from a pocket. "Right here."

Amelia grimaced as she glanced from one pair of cuffs to the other. "What do we do?"

Axel unsnapped the bands and walked them over to Betty. "I'm going to place these on Betty. Pepper"—his gaze flickered to me—"try to reach her. These bands should act as an amplifier. Under normal circumstances the cuffs will allow you to connect better with an animal. Since here you're trying to establish initial connection, you may have to work harder."

"I understand."

Axel scooped Betty into one hand. Her short legs spindled as she pawed the air. He gently settled her on a table and placed the cuffs over her.

"There's no way to secure them," Axel said. "They'll just have to remain that way."

"What do you want us to do?" Amelia said.

"Moral support." Axel pointed to Betty. "Send good vibes. This may feel uncomfortable for her, so we need to focus good energy toward your grandmother."

"A lot's riding on this." I shook out my hands to loosen up. "Mattie said she couldn't communicate with her." I bit my bottom lip. "We need to establish a connection. Otherwise I'm afraid…"

"It'll be fine," Axel said firmly. "Fine. Don't doubt."

I blew a staggering breath from my lungs, lifted my chin and raised my chest. "Okay. I'm ready."

Axel's gaze hit each of us. "Is everyone else?"

Amelia and Cordelia nodded. His gaze flashed to me. "Then let's go."

FOURTEEN

"*U*m. How do I use these?"

I stared at the cuffs and suddenly realized I actually had less than no idea of what I was supposed to do with them. I mean, it was one thing to tighten a connection with Axel if he was wearing the bands, and something completely different to attempt to connect with my mute grandmother trapped in a toad's body.

Wasn't it?

Yes. It was.

"Try to reach her like you normally would," he said gently. "Do what you would in any other circumstance."

That would actually mean I would grab a chocolate bar and watch someone else do the work.

Kidding. Kidding.

I closed my eyes and focused on Betty. The bands' effects were immediate. Magic swelled in me, and I felt a rush of power. Yet at the same time all the magic became focused as if it had one primary task.

I was the person to create that task.

Betty? I launched the words at her like a missile. It was nearly a scream I was so desperate to talk to her, hear her smart mouth refer to me as *kid* and watch her light up her corncob pipe.

It was all I wanted.

Betty, can you hear me?

The power was working. How could it not be? It felt like someone had stuck my entire body in a light socket and filled me with a jolt of magic.

But still it wasn't working. I focused on the bands and willed them to churn out more power. To burn more magic.

Power flared. It filled the room, taking up its own space and seeming to breathe its own air.

Betty!

More silence.

I blinked and caught Axel's glance. "I can't reach her. I don't know what else to do."

He folded his arms. Biceps like concrete swelled through his shirt. "More. Use all the power."

"But I'll burn them up." Meaning the cuffs.

He shrugged. I tried not to feel the sting of his nonchalance, but it did hit hard. I told myself he did care about connecting with me when he was a werewolf but right now finding Betty was more important. Saving her was the one thing we needed most.

I closed my eyes and pushed, shoved, yanked and pulled. The room was so thick with magic I could've plucked it from the air and threw it into a stew.

Betty, can you hear me?

Pepper?

Hope flared in my chest. I pushed the bands to burn more power. *Betty! We need the potion. The recipe. You're trapped!*

Pepper I'm forgetting—

A loud crack splintered the air. My eyelids flared open. The bands on Betty had popped off. Mine were smoking and ready to ignite.

"Oh no!" I flipped them off my wrists right before they burst into flames. They fell to the floor. The leather curled and charred as it was consumed.

Axel tossed the cuffs covering Betty atop mine. They smoked.

Orange fingers shot out underneath. The cuffs burst into flames with a *swoosh*.

And then they were gone as if they'd never existed to begin with.

The room smelled of smoke and burnt leather. I exhaled a sharp breath. I glanced at Axel. He shook his head and frowned as if the whole thing were a doggone bad shame.

Cordelia clapped her hands. The candles flickered out, and the lights blinked on. "Well? What did she say?"

"Or did she say anything?" Amelia said.

"Of course she said something," Cordelia snapped. "This is Betty we're talking about."

I pressed my temples. "It was hard to reach her. But when I finally did, she said something about forgetting."

Panic filtered through Amelia's voice. "Forgetting who she is?"

"Forgetting the potion spell?" Cordelia offered much more calmly.

"I don't know." I cringed under the weight of their stares. "I'm sorry but she didn't say anything more. She didn't reveal what it was."

"So it could be anything." Axel lowered his hand from his lips. It was his classic thinking look. I tried not to ruminate on how sexy it was, especially under the circumstances, but it was pretty much impossible.

I studied Betty. Her color had returned, but she was unchanged. She looked as much like a toad as she had in the beginning.

"We don't have much choice then." I slid a hand down my jeans. My pockets were empty. Dang it. I could really do with a handful of jellybeans right about now. There was nothing like a handful of sugar to take the edge off a situation.

"What do you mean?" Amelia scooped up Betty and studied the toad. "What choices do we even have?"

"We have to find the poppet." My gaze cut to Axel. "Like ASAP."

He scrubbed his fingers through his scalp. "We need Garrick for that."

Another stranger thought struck me. "Or...we could maybe just wish her back to her old self?"

Cordelia's eyes flared. "And what makes you think that'll end up any better than what happened to your hair? Our grandmother will probably wind up a giraffe if you leave Amelia to the wishing."

"Very funny." Amelia glowered at Cordelia. "At least my wishing abilities weren't put on hiatus."

"I *asked* for it, in case you've forgotten." Cordelia turned to me. "Amelia's in the process of getting lessons from her father. I decided not to pursue my abilities—if I even have them—so I wished for my talents to be locked."

"By who?" I said.

"My dad," she said grudgingly.

I did my best not to laugh, but my best wasn't good enough. "I hope you're not getting cozy with him."

"Don't worry," Cordelia snipped. "I'm not."

Axel threaded his fingers through mine. "Before anyone makes a serious wish, why don't we do something simple?"

Amelia smiled brightly. "I can do simple. I love simple."

Axel whispered in my ear. "Wish for your hair color back."

I shivered as his breath tickled my flesh. "Okay. Amelia, I wish for my hair to return to its natural color."

Amelia brought her hands together like a caricature of a genie and snapped her head. "Your wish is my command."

Cordelia's hand flew to her mouth. "Oh God. It's…"

My hopes plummeted to the ground. "It's what?"

"It's fixable," Amelia shrieked. "It's totally fixable. That's what my dad says. Everything can be fixed."

Cordelia grimaced. "Well if by fixed you mean Pepper may have to shave her head and start over, then sure, it's fixable."

Now I was seriously freaking out. Like completely. I caught a glimpse of myself in the mirror and gasped.

Green. My hair was green. It was horribly, evilly slimy green. It was the color of algae or mold or mildew or gross baby pea poop.

It was green!

My breath came in ragged gulps. I was hyperventilating. Cordelia was right. I would have to shave it off and start over. I would have to buy a wig or hide in a cave for months.

"Don't panic." Axel's words floated into my ear.

I could not have an epic freak-out in front of him. "It's fine. It's totally fine."

He placed a hand on my shoulder. Warmth floated over my skin like I was being submerged in water.

"It's going to be fine," he murmured.

Then, starting at my scalp, the green vanished as red and gold washed down the tendrils like liquid fire. The mold and mildew dissolved and was replaced by my regular hair color.

I exhaled with relief. I hated to admit it, I really did, but if I had to walk around town with green hair, I would be the laughingstock of Magnolia Cove. No one would buy animals from me. It would be terrible.

When he was finished, Axel hooked a finger with mine. "It's only a glamour. Until Amelia can figure out how to return your hair color, this illusion will remain in place."

I sank my head to his chest. "Thank you."

He kissed my forehead. "You're welcome."

From behind I heard Amelia say, "Well, no one thanked me. I did my best to help. I think that deserves a little something."

"How about a little hint not to grant wishes?" Cordelia said. "Looks like your powers need to be put on hiatus, too."

I couldn't agree more.

I was dead tired by the time I hit my bed. I awoke stiff but ready to help Axel however I could.

New Year's was officially over, and it was time to return to work. Since I had a shopful of animals, it made the most sense for Betty and Hugo to come with me.

But first thing's first.

I showered, dressed, ate breakfast and headed out of the house with the intention of making a pit stop first. I'd texted Axel about where I was going, and he'd promised to meet me there.

Lucky enough, we arrived at the Magnolia Cove police station at the same time.

"How's the hair holding up?" He said.

I fluffed one end. "Perfect. Thank you."

We found Garrick Young in his office glancing over a stack of papers. He took one look at Axel and leaned back in his chair.

"So, Reign, what'd you uncover about the poppet?"

Axel and I took seats in front of the desk. I held Betty in a new box and had left Hugo with the desk sergeant.

"Rotten eggs make the sulfur smell," Axel said.

"Riddle me this, Reign." Garrick twirled a pencil between his fingers. "Why would you need rotten eggs if you have a poppet?"

"You need certain elements to bond a poppet to your target—hair, blood. But to actually make it work and if you want it to work powerfully—"

"Meaning cause death," Garrick interjected.

"Yes. If you want to kill someone using a poppet, then you have to use more. You need a spell, and that spell includes rotten eggs."

"And dragon's breath," I added. Garrick shot me a questioning glance. "We discovered dragon's breath is an ingredient in the spell."

Garrick nodded. "Ah."

"Not only that," I said, "but one of the potion contestants just about attacked Hugo the other day."

Interest filled Garrick's eyes. "You don't say." He tapped his fingers on the desk. "Tell me about that."

"Gale East, a former student at the Southern School of Magic, created a potion that finds magical creatures."

"What else?"

"She was expelled from the school," Axel offered. "Plus she checked out Keating's *Book of Spells*."

Garrick clicked his tongue. "I'm going to assume Keating has lots of information on poppets."

I smiled. "Right. So it's possible Gale East created a poppet of

Shelly Seay, possibly seeking revenge, then killed her and stole the potion."

Garrick rubbed the stubble on his chin. "Why steal the potion? I mean, we all know it's missing. But why would anyone take it?"

"Turn their worst enemy into a toad?" Axel offered. "I don't know. But I suggest you search her place."

"What am I looking for? A poppet?"

"For one," Axel said. "But she would've destroyed Shelly's by now. Just to be safe. I'd look for Shelly's potion."

Garrick scratched his head of thick brown hair. "And how will I know when I've found her potion? This East woman's place could be filled with vials."

"Betty," I said quickly. "She might be able to help. Maybe if you let her smell them or something, she'll be able to signal that it's the right potion."

The two men stared at me as if I'd grown five heads. They glanced at the toad, which sat like a lump of dirt in the box.

I had to sell this somehow. "I mean, it's not a perfect plan, but it's something."

Garrick's gaze shifted to Axel. "I've heard of crazier things."

"Me too, but this just might work." Axel stared at Betty. "It's about the best thing you've got."

"But it still doesn't explain why anyone would want the potion," Garrick mused. "Shelly Seay wasn't liked. I get that. Folks don't like sorcery of any sort. Shelly had to summon threats to teach witch defense. If anyone thought Shelly was using her abilities to conjure the dead, they might want to get rid of her; that much I can understand. But is it enough to kill someone over? She was fired a while back from the school. It wasn't like it was a recent thing."

"We don't know motives," Axel said. "We were only asked about the poppet."

Garrick sighed. "I know. And you've brought me enough information to at least search Gale East's house. I'll do that." He rose and plucked his fedora from a peg on the wall. "Pepper, can you come with me if I need you?"

I nodded. "I'll be at the shop. Just let me know when and where."

Garrick headed toward the door. "Keep your phone on. I'll be calling you."

I could hardly wait.

FIFTEEN

"**W**hy *would* someone steal the potion?"

Axel was driving me to Familiar Place. Betty sat in my lap, and Hugo sat in the back seat sticking his head out the window.

I pushed the heat up to high. "I don't know why anyone would want to turn people into toads unless there was someone they didn't like."

Axel's jaw clenched. "But how would they even know about the potion?"

"Shelly came to us. Maybe there were other people she approached about the potion. Or maybe the information leaked."

He tapped the steering wheel. "That's what I would bet on. Someone leaked it. Anyone behind us?"

I craned my head to look out the back window. "No one."

"Hold on."

He cut the wheel hard to the left, and we did a U-turn. I scrambled to grab the sissy bar. "Where are we going?"

"Back to the school. There's someone we need to talk to."

"Who?"

His eyes narrowed to slitty wedges of death. "Saltz Swift."

"Why?"

"You'll see."

～

SALTZ SWIFT'S secretary wasted no time escorting us into the potion master's office.

"You knew what Shelly Seay was working on." Axel didn't phrase it as a question. Somehow he'd figured it out.

The potion master leaned back in his leather chair and studied us with a gaze that should've fried us into cracklings—or pork skins, for those of y'all not familiar with the first term.

Saltz pressed his fingertips together. "Yes, I knew what Shelly was working on."

"How long did your affair last?" Axel glared at him. "Up until she died?"

"You're very perceptive, Reign." Saltz wagged a finger at Axel. "You should teach intuitive magic."

"I prefer the job I currently have—private investigator."

"Well, we can't get them all, can we?" He inhaled sharply. "But to answer your question, yes, Shelly and I remained quite close."

"How close?" I couldn't help it. I had to ask.

"We remained…intimate up until her death."

"So when did she stop teaching at the school?" I flipped my hair over one shoulder and started braiding it. "From what I understood, the two of you were having an affair, she got moved to teaching witch defense, ticked some parents off and was fired."

"More or less. The administration really had no other choice." Saltz steepled his hands. "But she was only officially released from the school's payroll about six months ago. Up until then she remained able to teach."

I frowned, confused. "But it seemed to me that most people thought she was a sorceress." I rubbed my temples. I wasn't being clear. "What I'm saying is that Shelly was let go for being a sorceress a while back even though she was only technically fired from the school recently."

"Exactly," Saltz said. "When she had to bring certain unsavory creatures to light in order to teach the children how to defend themselves…well then it became clear to the parents exactly what she was, or at least what they thought she was."

"And what was she?"

Saltz stiffened. "Shelly Seay was a good woman who had the right motives. She wasn't moved by money or prestige. She only wanted to push forward the craft."

Axel smoothed a crease in his jeans. "Did you know about the potion?"

"Yes."

My jaw dropped. "But that's not how you reacted at the contest. You made it appear as if Shelly was about to work black magic."

"It was part of the plan." Saltz rubbed his tired face. "All of it. Shelly wanted me to react as if what she was going to do was wrong, to make it more dramatic. Shelly loved the dramatic." He smiled whimsically. "But then of course she died and the potion was taken."

"Then tell us why someone would do that." Axel crossed his arms. "Why would a person steal a potion that can turn another person into a toad?"

"Revenge, maybe?" A slow smile curled on his face. "Wouldn't it be a wonderful revenge to change someone you didn't like into a toad?"

I shivered. "My grandmother is currently a toad, and I don't think it's wonderful at all. In fact I think it's horrible."

"You don't have a sense of adventure, Miss Dunn. But that's why I believe someone would steal it. Revenge. *What* revenge? I don't know. And *why*? I have no clue."

"Fair enough." Axel nodded. "Tell us about Gale East."

Saltz sighed. "Gale was the sort of student who liked to experiment with things. She wanted to learn dark magic, and Shelly, for what it was worth, helped her as much as she could. But even Shelly had her limits. When Gale was found trying to create a poppet of a fellow classmate, as you can understand, we couldn't have that at the school. She was expelled."

"Did she harm anyone?" I said.

"No." Saltz smoothed his hair. "I don't think Gale East is the type who wants to harm people."

"She nearly killed my dragon."

Saltz's brows shot to peaks. "Well perhaps I stand corrected." He rose and straightened his jacket. "Now if you'll excuse me, there are things I must do." He walked toward the door. "Miss Dunn, we do look forward to your series on familiars."

Surprise flashed in Axel's eyes. "So it's all set, then?"

I smirked. "Hardly," I muttered. "Mr. Swift—"

"Please, call me Saltz." He smiled like a weasel.

"Hmm. Saltz. Did Shelly leave anything here?"

He motioned down the hall. "Yes. Most of her office is intact. I did it as a favor to her. She was going to finally clean it out after the holidays."

A spark ignited in my chest. This could be it—the break we were waiting for. Unless he knew more. I squeezed the box holding Betty.

"Did Shelly share any of her potion recipe with you?"

Saltz straightened. "Sadly no, she did not. If she had, we wouldn't be in this predicament now, would we? But we are. No. The only rites I know to transmute are blood rites." He fished a set of keys from his pocket. "But if she did write her recipe anywhere, her office would be the most likely place."

He led us down a vacant hall. Saltz unlocked a thick oak door and pushed it open.

The office didn't look like one of a fired teacher at all. It was chock-full of books and papers, glass orbs and knickknacks.

"Take your time in here. Anthony, the custodian, will be around shortly. He can lock up for you." Saltz rolled his shoulders. "Now. Is there anything else I can do for you?"

I placed the box on the desk. "No. Not for me."

Axel shook his head. "Me neither. Thank you."

Saltz Swift left us alone.

Axel rested his hands on his hips. "Let's get searching."

I shoved up my sleeves. "I couldn't agree more."

It was incredibly naive of me to think that Shelly Seay would've left the potion recipe atop her desk with a smiley-face sticker pasted to it, but that's what I hoped to find.

Maybe it would be easy peasy to find what we were looking for and we'd save the day in less than an hour.

Two hours later we were still digging through files and knickknacks.

"How does one person have so much stuff in such a small space?" I grumbled. "Didn't she ever throw stuff out?"

Axel chuckled. "You have no appreciation for the old-fashioned art of mini-hoarding."

I shot him a dark look. "You're joking."

"I am."

I fisted a handful of papers and dropped them to the floor. "It's just a bunch of stuff. Old exams, future teaching plans—there's nothing personal in here at all."

Axel shoved a file drawer full of papers back in the cabinet. "I agree." He stood in the center of the room and gazed around. "Wait a minute."

"What?"

He winked. "Maybe there is something here after all." He reached above a bookcase and pulled down a triangular wooden box. The wood was polished to a high gloss. It looked silky, the sort of thing you'd want to touch and of course keep away from the prying hands of children.

"What's that?"

"It's a puzzle box."

I frowned. "You mean the sort of thing you find in hippie stores and Renaissance fairs?"

He quirked a brow. "I see you're not above some role play."

I swatted him. "I've gorged myself on turkey leg once or twice in my life. Is it a simple puzzle box?"

Axel turned it over. "Simple enough. You have to move the pieces in the correct order or whatever's inside will be destroyed."

"Oh, simple." I rolled my eyes. "Great. So we've got a puzzle box that may or may not hold the potion recipe, and my grandmother who is currently encased in the body of a toad."

Axel wrapped a hand over my shoulder. "It shouldn't be that hard to solve." He stared at it and started to slide a stick of wood out and then changed his mind and shoved it back in.

I shot him a smug smile. "I thought it was going to be so easy."

"Don't make fun. I need to study it and think about it." His eyes lighted on me. "Want to work on it tonight, over dinner?"

Time alone with Axel? That seemed the best idea ever. "Sounds perfect."

He peered out the door. "Here. Hide this in your purse so no one knows we've smuggled it out." I dropped it in my bag. "Go on toward the truck. I'll be right behind. I'm just going to take one more look around."

I started to snatch up Betty, but Axel took her from me. "I've got your grandmother."

I headed out, keeping my chin tucked down low so that I didn't look like I was stealing anything. It wasn't like I was anyway. Shelly Seay was dead.

Dead. If no one had come for the puzzle box by now, I doubted they ever would.

I reached the front entrance to the school when I spied Anthony.

"Hey there," he said.

"Hi." I waved and lunged forward to grab the door. My purse slipped from my shoulder, and to stop it from falling open and the puzzle crashing to the floor, I braced my hand on the wooden door.

"Ouch!" I pulled my hand away and saw a thick sliver of wood had splintered from the door and lodged itself in my palm.

Anthony was beside me like white on rice. He took my hand gently and pulled the splinter from my skin.

"Thank you. Oh, there's blood."

He stoppered the flow with a handkerchief. "That old door needs some repair work."

I shot it an evil glare. "I would say so. But it was my fault. I lost my balance."

He shook his head of curls. "Nah. It's old." He studied me. His small eyes peered out from behind plump apple cheeks. "What're you doing here?"

"Oh, just talking to Saltz Swift about…giving a few lectures. Listen, thanks for leading the potion talk."

He shrugged. "I like magic."

My gaze bounced around the school. "It must be neat working here."

He nodded. "I don't do much."

I squeezed his shoulder and smiled. "It seems you do a lot. You know a lot, and you've already helped me. I appreciate it."

He applied steady pressure to my wound. "So what potion did you create for the contest?"

"Oh, I—"

"Pepper!" Axel bounded down the hall. "You okay?" His gaze cut to Anthony.

I pulled my finger from the handkerchief. "Oh fine. I cut myself is all." I showed it to Anthony. "Look. It's not bleeding anymore. Thanks." My gaze flickered to the stain on the white fabric. "Do you want me to wash that for you? I'm sorry about ruining it."

He shook his head and tapped it. The stain vanished. "No need. See? Good as new."

Axel's arm curled around my bicep. "We need to go."

I thanked Anthony again and followed Axel. "What is it?"

A fire glinted in his blue eyes. "Garrick called me. He's at Gale East's going through her stuff."

I scoffed. The nerve of the sheriff. He was supposed to call us *before* they went in. "Nice of him to let us know."

"He is letting us know." Axel unlocked the Rover and opened the door for me.

I climbed in and latched my seat belt. "Let us know what?"

"They've found something." Then he shut the door.

SIXTEEN

*W*e arrived at Gale East's house a little while later. I didn't know what I expected, but I hadn't prepared myself for seeing Gale perched on her front porch, glaring at the officers as they entered and exited her house.

I sank into the seat. "I can't be here."

Axel killed the engine. "Why not?"

"Because I've established an almost friendship with her. I can't be seen walking into the house with the bad guys."

Axel smirked. "Good point. Stay here." He got out and entered the house. Gale shot a look toward the Rover. I basically melted into the seat so she wouldn't see me.

Listen, even though I was pretty certain she was guilty, I didn't want her to think that's what I really thought.

Betty stared at me with her yellow eyes. Hugo licked my head. "Okay, both of you. Listen, I can't go in there. I have to wait here and see what happens."

Turned out, I didn't have to wait long before Axel opened the door and slipped in.

"Scaredy cat." He fired up the engine.

"It's called self-preservation."

"It's called being afraid."

He pulled away from the street. "Well? What did Garrick have? What'd he find?"

"You'll see."

I sat up and adjusted the car seat. "What do you mean?"

"We're meeting him at the station. You'll see exactly what's going on."

~

"OH MY LORD."

I stared down at a beautifully carved wooden box full of wax figures of people. Some had real hair that looked like they had been yanked from a hairbrush. One had a bright red mouth similar to red lipstick.

"We found these in Gale's house." Garrick flicked a hand toward the box. "Poppets aren't my expertise, but I was wondering if y'all could figure out who they are and how old they are."

I gestured toward the one with the lips. "Shelly Seay wore that color lipstick."

"She did." Axel rubbed his chin. "I'm sure a lot of women do, though."

"Is there a way to test them? To know who they represent?"

"Unless they have DNA on them, no."

Garrick shifted his weight. "We can test the hair if we need to, but it'll take some time to get back from the lab."

I crossed my arms. "Strange that magic is instantaneous, but DNA results still take time."

"It's not magic." Garrick scowled something fierce. "That one looks really yellow, though."

"The one with the lips?" I said.

He nodded. "If Gale made a poppet of Shelly Seay a while back, why would she only just now be using it?"

"That's a good question." Axel drummed his knuckles on the desk.

"Maybe she didn't need it then," I offered. "Look, we know Gale was Shelly's mentee. Maybe Shelly instructed her in making the poppet."

Axel narrowed his gaze. He got a look on his face he only made when he was thinking wizardish sorts of thoughts. Like he was about to work a bucketload of magic or about to release a can of whoop-butt on the world. It was an expression that could make grown men cower.

Me, I liked it.

Axel folded his arms. "I think that's a question that only Gale can answer."

Garrick moved to the door. "Looks like I'll be talking to Miss East."

Axel and I left, as interrogating folks was pretty much police business and had absolutely nothing to do with us. Garrick promised to call Axel if he needed any more help with the poppets.

"That one sure did look like Shelly," I murmured. We were back in the truck and heading toward Familiar Place.

"A lot of women wear red lipstick," he countered.

"I agree. But there are lots of pieces clicking together. Maybe Gale will just admit she used the poppet to kill Shelly and tell Garrick where she hid the potion." I raked my fingers through my hair. "It has to be her, right?"

"It doesn't have to be." His head tipped toward mine. "But it could be, and you're right, all the pieces do fit together."

I sank back into the seat. "But you can't force them. They have to lock on their own."

"Like that puzzle box."

"Yep. Just like it."

He stopped in front of the store, and I hopped out along with Hugo and Betty. Well, Betty didn't hop. I carried the box under my arm.

We said goodbye, and I went inside Familiar Place. As soon as I opened the doors—a bit late, I admit—it seemed there was a rush of folks buying all sorts of things—supplies, food, pets, anything and everything.

The day zoomed by quickly. I was close to locking up when the door opened again.

Gale East stood in the frame.

I almost vomited.

"Gale, how're you? So glad to see you." I had to bite my tongue to stop from saying things like—*why weren't you arrested? Why do you have a poppet of Shelly Seay? Where's the potion, damn it? I need to fix my grandmother before she forgets she's my grandmother and remains a toad for the rest of her life.*

You know, just a few things. That was all I had on my mind.

"I'm not good." Her gaze flashed to the box. "The police. They came to my house today. They think I've done something horrible. But I haven't, Pepper."

"Um."

She peered at Betty the Toad. "Is that her? Is this your grandmother?"

"Yes, it is." I whisked the box away. "Sorry. But she's sort of stuck like this and vulnerable."

Gale wrung her hands. I have to admit the look of angst on her face was believable.

"They think I have Shelly's potion and that I killed her."

I licked my lips. Hmm. "Who? The police?"

"Yes!"

"Have they said as much?"

Gale raked her fingers through her thick Brillo hair. "No! Yes! No. Sort of. They found an old box of poppets I had."

I gasped because it seemed the right response. "Poppets! Why would you have those?"

She crumpled into a chair. Yes, by all means, kill a woman, keep a potion that could save my grandmother away from her and then sit in my chair as if you own the place.

Help yourself.

"Long ago I used poppets, but it was overseen."

"Oh?" I sank into a chair across from her. "By who?"

"By someone."

"Wasn't it Shelly?"

"Yes. No. Partly. Look, she got a bad rap as a sorceress when she summoned some dark stuff for the students to fight against, but no one was ever going to be hurt. Shelly wouldn't have allowed it."

"I see." I didn't see at all. Who had taught her how to make poppets? Was it Saltz? "Can I get you some water?"

"Yes." She slumped farther onto the chair.

I grabbed a small bottle from a fridge in the office and handed it to her. "Just take your time and explain it to me. Back at the contest you made it seem that you didn't like Shelly."

"I lied." She unscrewed the cap and nearly finished the pint in one swallow. Gale swiped an arm over her moist lips. "I've never had much luck in school. When Shelly Seay took me on as her mentee, I thought I was saved."

"Were you?"

Gale blinked as if startled. She reacted like it was the strangest question in the world. I considered it perfectly normal.

"No," she finally answered. "I wasn't saved. But I thought I was." She rubbed her palms over her hair. "I know I seemed like I didn't like Shelly, but that's only because things didn't end well between us."

The image of the poppet with bright red lipstick popped into my head. "Is this about the poppets?"

"The poppets are something else. I was so young when I made them. I kept them. I don't know why. It was stupid. Foolish of me. I wanted to see how far I could push my craft. See what all I could do."

She shook her head. "Then I made some for fun. I was never going to use them."

She crumpled over, and I squeezed her shoulder. "It's okay. We all make mistakes, but if you've done something that hurt another person, you should say so."

Gale slowly glanced up, and I nodded toward Betty. "There are other people's lives at stake. Shelly Seay can't be saved. It's too late for her, but it isn't too late for my grandmother."

Gale palmed tears from her eyes. "I wish I could help, but I don't know how. I'm innocent, Pepper. I know I've done some things in the past."

I fisted my hands. I wasn't buying into this whiny crap. There was more than enough reason to believe that Gale East was guilty of murder.

"You almost knocked out my dragon. I know for a fact that to control a poppet, one of the things you need is dragon's breath."

She shivered. "I know but I didn't do it. It wasn't me. There are other people who know more about poppets than I do. The person who taught me."

"Right. Who taught you?"

Her gaze darted to the floor. "I don't know if I should say."

I gripped her shoulders and was about to shake an entire world of sense into her. "What's wrong with you? A woman is dead."

"I can tell you, but I know he's innocent."

We'll be the judge of that. "Who is it, Gale?"

Her lips trembled. "The person who taught me how to make poppets is Bo."

My stomach fell. "Bo? As in Shelly's boyfriend?"

Gale swallowed loudly. "Yes. He taught me everything I know."

SEVENTEEN

"*G*ale said Bo taught her about poppets."

I thought Axel was going to drop the pan of stir-fried veggies on the floor.

"Can I help you with that?"

He straightened and righted the pan, sliding it back onto the stovetop. Axel yanked a towel from the counter, wiped his hands and flipped it over one shoulder.

"Bo?" he repeated. "Bo taught her? Bo, the man who let himself be turned into a toad?"

I nodded. "The one and same. That's what Gale said."

He pulled two glasses from the cabinet and filled them with water. "Bo. Huh. He doesn't strike me as quite that smart."

"Or quite that evil?"

He pushed a glass toward me. "You don't have to be evil to work poppets. Not necessarily."

That struck me as an odd thing to say. "Are you sure? I thought working with poppets is dark magic."

"It is. The darkest. Transmutation is close simply because of what you have to sacrifice in order to work the spell correctly." He divided the stir-fry between two plates.

"Thank you."

"You're welcome." He hopped on a seat beside me and handed me a fork and knife.

I bit into a crunchy carrot. "What a healthy treat."

"Glad you appreciate it."

"I do." My gaze snagged on him. Heat rose in my cheeks. What this man did to me. All he had to do was look at me and my heart pounded, my skin flushed and I couldn't remember how to speak.

Okay, the speaking part was an exaggeration, but you know what I mean.

He quirked a brow. "We should probably just keep this talk to food and not get carried away with ourselves."

"Who said I was going to do that?"

"You didn't. It was the look in your eyes. They held a certain something that insinuated a lot."

I stared at my plate. "I have no idea what you're talking about."

He laughed. "It's okay. It happens to me, too."

I rolled my eyes. "Okay. Anyway." Time to deflect and not talk about kissing and stuff. No time to even think about it. "What did you mean when you said a person doesn't have to be evil to use poppets?"

"Ah." He swiped a napkin over his mouth. "Poppets can be used for good."

"By some sort of poppet fairy? You're kidding, right?"

He smiled. The corners of Axel's eyes crinkled as amusement sparked in his eyes. "Oh, if only the world wasn't so complicated. It would be better if all poppets were bad and then there wouldn't be the gray, would there?"

"Are you being cryptic on purpose?"

"No. Here's the deal—poppets can be used to heal people."

Food nearly fell from my mouth. "To heal?"

"Yes." Axel took a bite of food and relaxed back onto his chair. He folded his arms and studied me. "That's why it took so long for some towns to make their use illegal—because they're traditionally used to heal."

"But then one bad apple screws everything for everyone else."

"Exactly."

I twirled my fork. "So they give poppets a bad name. It doesn't help that in order to really work the power of the poppet, the spell calls for some unsavory elements."

He draped his arm over the back of my chair. "I love rotten eggs. I don't know what you're talking about."

"Ha-ha. Very funny." I dropped my fork onto my plate. "That was delicious. Thank you."

"You're welcome."

Our gazes snagged again. The air pressure in the room changed. It thickened. I didn't know if it was imaginary or literally the magic inside us ratcheting up and causing the heaviness. The pressure compounded, making my head swim. The power needed to release.

It did when Axel kissed me. It was deep and passionate and tasted of stir-fry. I sighed into him, and in return his hand glided to my cheek.

When we parted, he whispered into my mouth, "I'm sorry I ever left."

"I'm just glad you returned after your freak-out."

He chuckled and pulled me to him. "What would I do without you?"

"Live a miserable life."

"You're right about that." He leaned back and brushed a few strands of fake red hair from my face. "The color's holding up great."

I frowned.

"What is it?"

"I don't want to have to use a glamour to keep my hair luscious and beautiful forever. I hope Amelia can fix it."

He clipped my chin with his fist. "You don't need a glamour for your hair. You are luscious and beautiful no matter the color." He leaned back and studied me. "Wait. Are you blushing?"

Pretty sure every inch of me burned bright red. "Um. I don't know what you're talking about."

He tipped his head back and stared at the ceiling. "What you do to me. I can't even think straight."

I curled my fingers into his shirt. "Who says you have to think?"

He unhooked me. "I have to think. A lot's happening in the next few days. The moon will be full soon."

"Oh dear Lord! I almost forgot." Axel turning into the wolf was almost the worst timing ever. We needed to fix Betty, find the potion—well not in that order. We had to get the potion and then fix Betty. If we happened to catch a murderer in the meantime, then so be it.

But I couldn't hide the panic from my voice. "When are you turning? Tomorrow? What do you need me to do?"

"Hold on there." He raised a hand for me to stop. Axel threaded his fingers through mine and led me to the couch.

"The plates?"

"We'll clean up later."

"Like tomorrow?"

Not that I was hoping things would go far, but I didn't mind a little kissing time with Axel. If that kissing lasted all night, then well, that's what happened.

"I'm changing day after tomorrow."

Whew. "Okay. Well that gives us plenty of time to figure out how to save Betty." I sank onto a cushion and hiked an arm over the neck of the couch. "So you think the new place you built will hold you?"

"It's not the house I'm worried about."

"What then?"

"You."

I blanched. "Er. Hey. So I was thinking about Betty. Do you think we could maybe work a transmutation spell to save her?"

He tilted his head back and laughed. "Way to change the subject."

"I have no idea what you're talking about."

Axel shot me a hard look. "Right. But anyway, first of all there's no way to know if a transmutation spell would actually work since Betty was changed with a potion. We did try a modified one, and since it wasn't successful, that is my guess as to why. Secondly, Betty wouldn't approve of such a spell because of the ritual sacrifice."

I cringed. "Yeah. That's what I thought."

He lifted my feet and started to knead the tender insole. "You wouldn't approve either. You want to sacrifice a cat?"

I grimaced. "No. That's disgusting."

"That's how it was done. But anyway…"

I batted my eyelashes. "Yes?"

"I was wondering about the potion you made for the contest."

"Ah, the ever so elusive potion. Oh yes, that spot right there." I moaned and sank farther into the couch. "Don't ever stop. Can I take you with me everywhere I go so you can continually massage my feet?"

"No." His tone might've been flat, but the twinkle in Axel's eyes had mischief written all over it.

I laughed. "Way to be honest."

"I stayed out of your way when you worked here, but I have a feeling I should know what the potion was."

I rolled my eyes. "What makes you say that?"

"It has to do with animals. I know that much."

"You think you're so smart." He stared at me until I folded. "Yes. It has to do with animals. I thought that along with the arm cuffs, I could connect with you."

He nodded. "Ah. I knew it had something to do with me."

"You're incorrigible," I teased.

He winked. "I know I am." He shook his head. "Were you going to tell me?"

"Actually I was going to drug you when you weren't paying attention."

He laughed. "Sounds like a perfect plan."

"No. I was. Listen, I think we can do this. I think if I can connect with you by using the potion, you'll have a real shot at a breakthrough."

He quirked an ebony brow. "You don't want to use it on Betty?"

"It's not that kind of potion. It's supposed to take the connection that's already there and make it stronger. Besides…" I glanced at the floor. How could I really tell him? It was so embarrassing. But of course I'd created it for him, so I would have to tell him at some point.

Axel dropped my feet to the floor and leaned in. He extended a hand and lifted my chin until our gazes locked. "Yes? Besides what?"

"Besides, it's geared toward werewolves specifically. It's not for another creature, so I don't think it'll work. There have to be plenty of other folks who want to communicate with werewolves."

"Tame them, you mean."

I shook my head. "No. I'm not trying to tame you. I'm not trying to tame anyone. I want you to be in control. That's all. That's all I've ever wanted."

He slid a hand over my cheek. "Sorry, that came out wrong."

"It sure did. That's not what you think, right? That I want to control you?"

He rubbed his face and sighed. "Pepper, we've been through this. I'm a beast."

"But you don't have to be! Your father isn't."

"That's different. It's taken him years to establish that connection with my mother. It's not as if it happened overnight. Besides, I just think…I think there's more beast in me."

"That makes no sense. He's full-blooded werewolf; you're only half."

"I learned some things when I left."

"When you abandoned us."

He squinted. "I thought you forgave me."

I cringed. *Great thing to say, Pepper.* "I do. I just don't want you to forget."

"Are you punishing me?"

"No." I rubbed my face. "No. Sorry. It just still hurts."

He lifted my hand and kissed the inside of my wrist. I shivered as a pulse of heat bled over my skin. "I'll never forget. But when I was gone, I learned a few things about the wolf inside me. Most of which was that I'm more feral than most. I'm not saying my father isn't a fighter or an alpha; all I'm saying is that the blood runs hotter in some people than others."

"And it runs hotter in you." Realization sparked in my head. "That's why we've been able to establish a connection before but it's never lasted."

He nodded. "I think that's right. You have to believe me when I say that's all I want. That more than anything I want us to be connected." He pressed my hand to his chest. His heart beat steadily under his shirt. "I don't want to be a slave to the beast. I want control. But Pepper," he said with a sigh, "I don't know if I'll ever have it."

I grabbed his hands. "You have to believe otherwise." Tears stung my eyes. It was so stupid. Why was I crying? Because I wasn't giving up but Axel was?

He slid his thumb over my cheek. "This potion of yours. I'll try it as long as it won't kill me."

I hiccupped as laughter bubbled in my throat. "I don't think it'll kill you, but I can't make any promises."

"Well as long as you don't *think* it'll do me in, that's enough for me." He grinned widely. It was contagious. I smiled back.

"It won't. I'm pretty sure." I wrapped my arms around his waist and hugged tightly. So tightly I was surprised Axel didn't pry me from him and wonder who the madwoman was who'd leeched on to him.

It was true though; I didn't want to let go. I rubbed my lips over his thick cotton shirt and inhaled his scent.

"Thank you for believing in me," I whispered.

He wove his fingers through my hair. "No. It's I who needs to thank you. You've never given up on me. I owe you a lot for that. The least I can do is drink the potion. But I won't just drink it. I'll believe in it."

"I hope it works." I squeezed him again.

"Me too."

We lay like that for a while. I started getting tired.

"We forgot about the puzzle box," I murmured.

"It can wait," Axel whispered.

I must've fallen asleep because the next thing I knew I was back in my own bed, the sheets pulled to my chin and the sun streaming through the windows.

Amelia shook my leg. "Pepper, wake up."

I rubbed my eyes and yawned. "Good morning."

"Morning." She clenched and unclenched her teeth. Amelia's anxiety practically busted through the ceiling. I frowned and pushed myself up. "What is it?"

She tugged my arm. "Come on. I've got something to show you."

EIGHTEEN

$\mathcal{I}$ rubbed goopy sleep crap from my eyes and followed Amelia down the stairs. Hugo and Mattie were already there. Hugo had draped himself across the rug. He opened his mouth, and a short burst of fire streamed forth.

"Hugo," I chided. "Not in the house."

He dropped his head to the floor.

"Sugar, dragon fire is the least of your worries."

"What is it?"

Amelia rubbed her hands with all the guilt of Lady Macbeth. "I was trying to help. I thought that maybe my wishing skills were getting better. I managed to grant one of my dad's yesterday."

Fear spiked down my spine. "What did you do?"

"See, I was trying to make things better." Amelia cringed. "But I'm afraid I made them worse."

"Okay," I said slowly, "I understand that. But you need to tell me what you did so that we can see if things can be fixed."

But Amelia wouldn't spit it out. "I just saw a need and tried to fill it. I wanted to help. I'm a helpful person."

"We all know that." I shot a look to Mattie. "Don't we know that?"

"We sure do, sugarbear. We all know how much Amelia wants to help."

I reached for my cousin. "What is it?"

She shrank three sizes as her spine bowed. "Promise you won't be mad?"

No. "Yes."

Amelia moved away from the dining table.

I gasped. "What did you do?"

"You promised not to be mad!"

I stared at her as if she had three heads. "I'm not mad. I'm really not."

"I would be mad," Mattie said.

Amelia nibbled her fingernails. "You're not?"

"No. I'm not mad. There aren't words to describe exactly what I am, but mad isn't one of them."

But then the words hit me—horrified, astounded, defeated, *homicidal.* No, I wasn't angry with my cousin.

I was furious.

"How could you have done this?"

Amelia pressed her balled hands to her cheeks. "I know! I'm sorry. I don't know. It just…I'm sorry."

"It's not me you should be apologizing to. It's Betty."

Betty the Toad sat on the floor beside the table. Her gullet pulsed, and her eyes blinked.

"What happened?" It was horrible.

Amelia approached Betty. "I thought maybe if she was bigger, that maybe things would work out."

"She had me wish that Betty was back to her normal size." Mattie jumped on the table. "And this is what happened."

A five-foot toad squatted in the middle of the floor. Betty was Betty-sized all right, but she was still an amphibian.

"Why didn't you just have Mattie wish her back to herself?" I couldn't believe Amelia would be so careless. "Besides, wasn't it already discussed that wishing wouldn't work?"

"Yes," she squeaked. "But I wanted to try."

"Well you tried all right."

And failed miserably. How could Amelia do this? She knew her wishes weren't ready to be granted yet.

I pressed my palms to my temples. "You did this because of Cordelia, didn't you?"

"Maybe."

I shot her a scathing look. "You might as well just admit it. Did you do this because you wanted to prove to our cousin that she's wrong about your dads and about your powers?"

Amelia sank onto a chair. There was no denying how miserable she looked. I knew my cousin was sorry, but why? Why would she have asked Mattie to do this?

I raked my fingers through my hair, relishing the feel as my nails scraped my scalp. The stress was building up in me, and I needed some sort of release.

"I'm afraid of what she's going to eat now." Amelia trembled as she glanced at Betty.

"It's still Betty in there."

Amelia shuddered. "I don't know. I don't think so. Pepper, I hate to say it, but I think she's gone."

I sighed. My cousin had only been trying to help the situation. Granted she'd made it worse, but at least she was doing *something*. I had to give her credit for that—like maybe I'd make Amelia her very own pan of dressing next Thanksgiving.

I mean, who doesn't want an entire pan of dressing? I know I would snatch that up mighty quick.

I exhaled a shot of air. "Okay. Since this is the situation, we need to do something about it. Let me call Axel."

"No," Amelia wailed. "I don't want anyone to know."

I nearly fainted. "Oh Amelia, I think we'll be lucky if the entire town doesn't find out. *Lucky*. This is so bad. We need help. I don't know how to deal with this."

"Yes, you do. You can turn her back."

"Amelia, you and I both know witchcraft can't mingle with genie magic. It won't work." I snapped my fingers. "Your dad and uncle. Call them?"

She slumped off the chair, shoulders hunched, as she made her way to her purse and called them.

Within minutes Morgan and Bean had arrived. I didn't know how they made a living, but I was glad their schedules were so flexible.

Bean surveyed Betty. "What happened?"

Mattie answered. "That daughter of yours had me make a wish that Betty was back to normal size, and now look at her—she's a giant toad."

Morgan's hands twitched. "Well at least she isn't any bigger. This is something we can deal with."

Hope filled Amelia's eyes. "You think?"

Bean squeezed her shoulder. "I think Morgan's right. But here's the deal—no more granting wishes unless we're around. You're simply not ready for it."

She agreed. "I'm not. I know that."

Morgan shot her a wide smile. "It's fun though, granting them. But sometimes this is what happens."

"Things go wrong, sweetheart. Especially in the early days of using your power." Bean gazed at Amelia gently, as if she were an injured animal.

I realized then exactly how much her dad loved her. Both Morgan and Bean had never wanted to leave their daughters. But for the safety of their girls, there'd been no other choice.

"And we don't know how your chaos witching mothers affect you," Morgan said. "I'm sure they've got some kind of influence, but we don't know exactly what."

Bean nodded toward Betty. "But right now let's focus on this problem and see if we can turn your grandmother back to normal."

"Yeah, before she eats me," Mattie said. "I don't like the way that toad's been eyeing my thighs."

I grimaced. Mattie was right. Betty did glance around the room, but there was something oddly vacant in her gaze. Something had vanished, like my grandmother. I couldn't see her in those eyes anywhere.

I wanted to crumple on the ground. But instead I locked my knees and shoved my shoulders back. "Let's see if we can get this solved. There's somebody I need to speak to."

Morgan's gaze slid to me. "Wish for her to return to frog size."

My stomach knotted. "Is this going to work?"

"As well as anything." Bean moved some chairs away from the table. "Just make sure your intention is clear when you make the wish."

"So don't think about her returning to Betty."

"Right," Morgan said. "Just wish her back to the way she was earlier."

I threaded my fingers together and cracked my knuckles. "Here goes nothing." I inhaled a deep shot of air. "I wish that Betty would return to regular toad size."

Morgan nodded his head. "As you wish."

Glittery magic whirled in the air. It circled Betty, and in the blink of an eye she'd returned to normal.

Well, sort of.

She was still a toad after all.

I slumped into a chair. "Thank goodness. I'm so glad she's okay." I shook a finger at Amelia. I felt guilty shaking a digit at my cousin, but she'd been incredibly irresponsible. And not ditzy irresponsible, just plain old out-of-character bad.

"No more wish granting."

She shrank. "I won't."

"I mean it." It shot from my mouth as a growl.

Amelia flinched. "You're right. I'm sorry."

Bean placed a gentle but firm hand on my shoulder. "We'll make sure she doesn't do it again." He nodded to his brother. "Perhaps we need to lock down your powers until you have a chance to really learn them. We'll give both you girls lessons and take it slow."

"Okay," she whimpered.

I hated to say it, but I had no sympathy for Amelia. Not right now. "Can y'all take care of Betty?"

Morgan nodded. "We'll make sure she's okay."

"Great. I've got some things to do."

"Do you think you could snatch the poppet from Garrick's office?"

"Since when did you start committing crimes?"

I'd opened Familiar Place on time, thank goodness, and had called Axel, who came over.

The store was full of yapping, chirping animals. I raised my voice so I could be heard about the chatter. "It's not that I want to commit a crime, but we need to force a few things. Like, what did Garrick say when you told him that Gale accused Bo of being the person who introduced her to poppets?"

"He said he'd look into it."

"Not good enough." I curled my fingers into the back of a chair. "It's not good enough. We need results now. There's no more time to waste."

He rubbed my back. "I'm sure it'll be fine. I know you seem to think that Betty is slipping away, but if she's inside, she won't forget. She's just trapped, Pepper. That's all. It will be fine."

I jerked away. "You weren't there. You didn't see a giant toad-Betty staring blankly at me. Axel, we're losing her. We've got to get that potion or find a replacement or sacrifice something."

"You don't mean that."

"I'm desperate!"

The animals stopped all jabbering and stared at me. I lowered my voice. "I'm desperate. We need a miracle and Christmas is over."

He nodded. "Okay. I'll see what I can do."

Axel kissed my forehead and left. I sank onto a chair.

The animals immediately started back up. *What's wrong?* meowed a kitten.

She looks sad, dummy, retorted a puppy.

I know she looks sad, spat the kitten.

Tell us what's wrong, Pepper, said a parrot.

We want to help, yelped a puppy.

I dropped my head to the counter. "My grandmother is a toad. The one I brought in before. She's become a toad and there's no way to help her except this stupid potion that this one woman made and I don't have the potion and I don't have a way to save Betty unless one of you wants to become a ritual sacrifice and I don't want that to happen to any of you."

I took a deep breath. "So I can't save her. She's slipping away, becoming more like a toad every day. Heck, if we ever do find the potion, she'll probably be so far gone there won't be a way to bring her back. It's horrible. Absolutely horrible and I don't expect any of you to be able to help."

Of course by this time I was sobbing. I grabbed a tissue box, yanked out several tissues and blew my nose something fierce.

You talking about a potion that turns people into toads? It was a kitten again.

"Yes, I'm talking about that stupid potion. Why did she have to do it?" I stared up at the ceiling accusingly. "Betty, why did you let Shelly talk you into the potion?"

Oh, that's easy, said the parrot. *Your grandmother let Shelly talk her into it.*

"But why?"

Because Shelly had something the old lady wanted, a puppy said.

I stopped and stared at the group. This was getting weird and making no sense. A chill trickled down my spine. My gaze dragged from the puppies to the cats and back to the birds. The animals eyed me expectantly, as if I was about to reveal some deep, dark secret.

"And how would you even know that? About Shelly having something Betty wanted?"

Because we were here when they made the potion, the parrot said.

The world stopped. It tipped to one side. Every coherent thought slipped from my brain. My mouth dried, and I swallowed a few times to work up the saliva for words to form.

I rose and crossed to the parrot. "I'm sorry. Can you say that again?"

I said, we were here when Shelly and Betty made the potion.

I swallowed a knot in the back of my throat. "Do you think you could remember the recipe?"

It was a long shot. One so long I nearly crossed my legs along with my fingers. My hair nearly stood on end when the parrot answered.

Yes.

NINETEEN

I rolled up my sleeves. "Okay. What do we need?"

They all shouted at once—*a rose kissed by a frog, newt eyes, frog's breath, warts from a speckled toad.*

There was more. There were so many ingredients I grabbed a pen and jotted as quickly as possible.

"Slow down!"

They didn't. In fact, I think they shouted faster.

Legs from a bat, said a turtle.

They didn't use them, remember, barked a puppy. *They substituted for fur from a black cat.*

"Does anyone have anything else?" Silence filled the air. "Anyone want to offer any other ingredients?"

No, squawked a parrot. *We don't have anything else.*

I ripped the sheet from a notebook and hugged it to my chest. "Do you remember the order?"

The animals stared at one another. Which, let me confess, did not make me feel very good about what they were going to say. Long stretches of silence didn't bode well in my opinion, but what did I know?

"So is everyone in agreement? Is this right?"

Finally a macaw answered. *It's correct! It's correct! But just to be sure, tell us again.*

I bit back my frustration and went down the list line by line. When I finished, I took a deep breath and gazed at every animal in turn. "Can anyone remember anything else? Anything at all?"

They shook their heads.

I took one last look at the page before folding it and pressing it to my chest. "Okay. Time to see if we can make some magic."

"THEY WENT through the potion at Familiar Place."

Axel was back at his house, and my nerves were stretched so thin I was surprised they hadn't snapped off and slapped someone in the face.

"Who went through the potion?"

"Betty and Shelly."

He quirked a dark brow. "How do you know that?"

"The animals told me."

Every muscle in his body tightened. At least the muscles I could see. Not sure about the ones I couldn't see. But those probably tightened, too.

"They worked the spell?"

I pulled the paper from my pocket and unfolded it. "Yes, and the animals told me the ingredients. They all agreed." I had to stop myself from shoving the slip of paper up under his nose. "This is the ingredient list."

His gaze swept down the sheet. "I have most of these things. The others we can get at the supply store, Magical Elements." He tapped a finger to his lips. "It's an interesting potion. I wouldn't have put some of these things together, but I'm not surprised it worked. Hmm. Maybe Shelly Seay was smarter than any of us gave her credit for."

"She used to teach potions at the school—before Saltz Swift came in, remember?"

He sank back. "Before I forget." He pulled the wax poppet with the red lips from a box. "Voila!"

I curled my fingers around the wax form and then shrank back. "I don't want to hurt it."

"You have to know who you're hurting before you can do that."

"Oh good." I threw my arms around his neck. "But you got it! That's awesome. Hopefully we won't need it. Fingers crossed we can release Betty with the potion."

Axel gently pushed me back. "And what sort of reward do I get?"

I perched up on my tiptoes and kissed his lips. "How's that?"

A slow smile crept over his lips. "I'll take it."

We stared at each other for a long moment before I hooked a finger into his shirt. "Well? What are we waiting for? We've got Betty to save."

Gathering the ingredients took less time than I'd thought. We decided to build the potion back at Familiar Place so the animals could talk us through it.

I could've done without a couple of animals, like the squawking parrots and meowing kittens, but the shop was really the best place to work.

It was quiet and my cousins' prying eyes wouldn't be anywhere near. Not that they were nosy, but after this morning I didn't want to raise anyone's hopes of finding a cure for Betty.

After all, it didn't seem like anything was going to work, least of all a potion with instructions from a bird.

I stared at the box of glass vials, most of which contained things so gross I didn't want to think about it. "What happens first?"

"First we start a fire." Axel stretched out his arms. When his hands met in a thunderous clap, a cauldron snapped into place in the middle of the room.

A fire burned green beneath it. "Magic fire," he explained as I eyed him incredulously. "It's different from the fire in your hearth."

"Well, obviously. That fire keeps all of Magnolia Cove magical."

He nodded. "This is magic fire for potion making. It helps infuse the ingredients with more power, more magic as it were."

I rubbed my hands. "Great because I am all about more magic."

He chuckled. "Okay. You have Betty?"

I pulled her from the box. "Cordelia and Amelia had no problem parting with her." I set the toad on the counter. "In fact, I'm pretty sure Amelia's glad to be rid of her. She doesn't like being reminded of her mistakes."

He tipped his head down. A dark expression as if my words had flared some sort of ancient memory flashed over his perfect features. "Who does?"

"I suppose no one."

"Okay. What happens first?"

A cacophony of spritely animal voices filled my ears. "They're saying to add all the liquids first."

Axel uncapped the first vial. "How much?"

Through the chatter I heard the amount and relayed it to him. "They said it's the same amount for each component."

"Interesting."

I sidled up beside him and peered into the cauldron. "How's it interesting?"

"It suggests a balanced potion. Potion work is sort of like communicating with universal magical law. Different amounts of ingredients signify different things. For instance less bat's wing than cat's whiskers suggests the slinking of a cat is more important in a potion."

"Hmm. This magic stuff gets stranger all the time."

He nudged me playfully with his shoulder. "It is fascinating and complex. It's more intuition than it is scientific, though there is a bit of science in it. Otherwise it wouldn't work."

He slowly measured and added ingredients. I considered offering to help, but my nerves were frayed. I'd probably do more harm than good in my current state.

"Tell me." Axel uncorked another vial. "Why did Betty decide to go along with Shelly? Do the animals know?"

"They said Shelly had something Betty wanted." I cocked my head toward the parrot. "What did Betty want from Shelly?"

The parrot flapped his wings. *A promise.*

I frowned. "What promise?" Axel shot me a confused look. I shrugged. "That's what the bird said."

That she wouldn't sell the potion, a kitten meowed.

"Wait. What?"

That's right, the parrot cawed. *The tall woman promised not to sell the potion if Betty went through with it.*

I curled my fingers into Axel's arm. "They're suggesting that Shelly was going to sell the potion, but Betty made her promise not to. It was the only way Betty would go through with being transformed."

Axel pulled his hair from his face and tied it back. "A potion like this in the wrong hands could be disastrous. Change all your enemies into toads and never return them."

"But couldn't you change them back if you used black magic?"

"Yes, probably. There's no guarantee. You'd be sacrificing something without the promise that it would work. Betty's smart. She realized that getting Shelly's word on that was more important than not being a guinea pig for the potion."

I slid onto the counter and stared at the cauldron. "But now someone else has the potion."

He nodded. "Now they do."

"And we don't know who."

"Hopefully it won't matter. It's not as if the sky is raining toads." Axel grabbed another vial. "We may not even have to worry about it."

A chill filled the room, and I rubbed my shoulders. "Maybe not. Maybe it's just all pure coincidence."

Axel's gaze snagged mine. "You don't think that."

"No but it's nice to dream."

He ignored my comment and grabbed the next vial. "Okay. How much of the dry ingredients?"

I asked the animals and relayed the information. He worked silently. I watched but couldn't stop thinking that someone had the potion. Perhaps they were simply waiting for the right time to use it. Of course, maybe Axel was right and they weren't going to use it at all.

Somehow that didn't feel right. I wished it were true, but my gut coiled and knotted, telling me something was wrong.

Axel turned to me and presented the finished product. "It's all done."

I peered into the cauldron. "That's it?"

"That's it," he said proudly. "Unless we're missing an ingredient."

"I don't think so. I went over the list with them twice." I stared at the baby blue liquid. "So that's supposed to work, huh?"

"That's what they said."

"I don't know. It doesn't look like the right color."

Axel frowned. "It was more golden, wasn't it?"

"It was like liquid sunshine. Nothing like this."

His gaze flickered to the animals. "Ask them what we're missing."

So I did.

We told you everything, a kitten said.

There's nothing else, barked a puppy.

"What about you?" I nodded to the parrot. "We've dropped in everything you've said, but something isn't right."

The parrot flapped his wings and flew to the table where we'd set the whiskers and wings, eyes and breath. He peered through the glass and inspected each and every vial.

They're all right, he cawed. *Every one.*

"But something's off."

Maybe you don't believe enough, said a kitten.

Yeah, maybe you've lost your Christmas spirit, added a puppy.

I flared my arms. "This is not Peter Pan. I'm not going to make a wish over pixie dust and have this thing turn out right. There's no way."

Axel sighed. "There probably was pixie dust added."

"What are you talking about?"

"Betty's blood."

My breath caught. "What?"

He scrubbed his knuckles down his cheek. "Shelly might've tailored the potion to Betty. The only way to do that would've been to use at least a drop of her blood."

I turned to the animals. "Well? Do you remember any blood?"

They were silent.

"It doesn't look good," I said to Axel.

"It's the only thing I can think of that's missing. It makes sense. It wouldn't have been a sacrificial potion, but to do a transmutation spell, you might still need blood."

I glanced at the toad. "So are you saying we have to prick her?"

"I'm afraid so."

"I'll hold her. I'm not doing any pricking. No matter what."

"I wasn't going to ask you to."

I exhaled a shot of air. "Good because there's no way I'm going to draw blood from Betty. Do you have any idea what sort of heck I'd have to pay for once we returned her to normal?"

He chuckled. "I'm sure she'd be grateful."

I cocked a brow. "Do you know Betty Craple?"

"Good point." Axel touched his fingers together. When he pulled them apart, a silvery needle hovered between them. "So I get the privilege."

I gestured toward the toad. "She's all yours."

"Help me hold her."

We shuffled Betty over to the cauldron. I closed my eyes as Axel pricked her foot.

"Blood makes me queasy. At least Betty's blood does."

"Chicken."

As much as I wanted to keep my eyes closed, I had to see. I had to know what was going to happen. I mean, we were saving Betty. Axel and I would be heroes.

Not that I was doing this so I could be adored by Magnolia Cove society. Absolutely not.

But I was doing it to earn brownie points with Betty. One could always use as many good points with her as possible.

I wasn't above admitting that.

A drop of blood dripped into the mixture. The potion contracted, as did the air in the shop. The room seemed to suck in and quickly expand as the potion shimmered.

The pressure returned to normal, and I exhaled a breath I didn't realize I had been holding.

"What was that?" I said.

Axel gently released his hold on Betty. I hugged her to me. "Sorry for hurting you," I murmured into her toad ear.

"That was the potion receiving the final ingredient." Axel winked at me. "Here goes nothing."

I glanced in the cauldron. The potion still wasn't quite the right color. It was close but just slightly off.

I set Betty on the counter. Axel ladled a spoonful of potion and placed it in front of Betty's nose. The toad spindled forward a step.

"Here goes nothing." Axel tipped the spoon. The potion slid down Betty's back. I wrung my hands, anticipating what would happen next.

TWENTY

I bit down on my lower lip so hard I was waiting for blood to bloom on it. Axel took my hand, and I grasped it while we waited for Betty to change.

And we waited some more.

I pressed at the worry line sprouting between my eyes. "Something isn't right. When Shelly turned Bo back into himself, it happened quickly. It didn't take this long."

"And when Betty became the toad, it was fast." Axel frowned. "You're right. Something is wrong. But what?"

Betty the Toad blinked at us. I raked my fingers down my face. "I'm so sorry. I thought we had it figured out." I glanced over my shoulder at the animals. "Thank you for your help. We wouldn't have made it this far without y'all."

The room buzzed with *you're welcomes*. My gaze flickered to Axel. "Should we wait a few more minutes?"

"I don't see why not." He threaded his fingers through mine. His touch gave me some comfort. Axel had a way about him. Often just seeing his smile not only made my heart soar, but it also filled me with warmth all the way to my toes.

I rested my head on his shoulder and sighed. "It's not going to work, is it?"

"No."

I released his hand and rubbed the heels of my hands to my eyes. "What are we supposed to do now? Wait for Betty to disappear into the toad and be lost to us forever?"

Axel took my hand and tugged me to him. He wrapped his concrete arms around me. I felt his lips brush the top of my glamoured hair.

Seriously, the New Year was not kicking off to a fabulous start. It pretty much sucked rotten eggs.

"Everything will be okay."

I tipped my head back and caught his gaze. "How can you be so sure?"

His grip tightened. "You forget—we have a poppet."

I almost jumped from his grasp. "Oh my gosh! That's right. We need to talk to Bo. You know where he lives, right?"

Axel's razor-sharp jaw hardened. "I know where he's been staying while in Magnolia Cove. He and Shelly had rented a place, and yep, he's still there."

"WE KNOW you taught Gale East how to make poppets."

Axel and I stood at Bo's front door. We'd clearly gotten him out of bed. He wore flannel pajama bottoms and a white T-shirt. His hair spiked around his head.

He rubbed his eyes and yawned. "What are y'all talking about?"

I yanked the poppet from my purse and threw it on the ground. "This is what we're talking about."

He shrank back. "Where'd you get that?"

"It's from Gale East's personal collection." Axel motioned to the doll. It rose in the air until it was eye level with Bo. "Looks a lot like Shelly, doesn't it?"

"I don't know what you're talking about."

Axel grabbed Bo by the collar and yanked him forward. "Would you like to start talking to me or do you want me to call the police?"

Bo cowered. "Okay. Okay. I'll tell you everything."

"That's better."

We followed Bo inside. Axel picked up the poppet and brushed it off. Bo pointed to a couch. Neither of us sat.

"Tell us everything," Axel demanded.

Bo sank onto a recliner. He scrubbed his hands over his hair and shook his head. "Yes, I taught Gale how to use poppets, but only because she asked me. Gale is trouble, okay? I don't know if you've figured that out yet."

"We know that Shelly took Gale under her wing."

"Right." Bo yawned. He sank back and folded his arms over his chest. "They became friends and Shelly taught her things but Gale wanted more. She wanted to know about poppets. Some kids were bullying her at school. Gale told Shelly, but Shelly just told her to hang in there. Shelly had a reputation as a sorceress, but she was a kind person."

Bo scraped a hand down his face. "Gale wanted a way to stop the bullying. I offered that."

"By showing her poppets? That's dangerous." I shook my head. Of all the ways to teach someone to deal with their problems, showing them how to use poppets to hurt someone was not the way to do it.

"I felt for her, okay?" Bo snapped. "The kid wanted help so I showed her."

"With a poppet that looks like Shelly, a woman who was just murdered." Axel voice sliced with accusations. "If I looked around, would I find rotten eggs in your house, too?"

Bo paled. "You never know when you'll need a rotten egg. There are spells that call for them."

Axel nodded. "There are. I just happen to know that commanding a poppet also calls for the use of rotten eggs."

"I didn't do it." Bo sighed. "Look, I taught Gale how to make poppets, I did. I admit it." He wrung his hands as if he were trying to come up with something, anything that would get him out of this.

"You think I didn't know about Shelly and Saltz? Everyone knew. Do you think I cared?"

"I would care," I said. Both men looked at me. I shrugged. "Well, I would."

"I didn't. I never cared about that. Who did Shelly come home to at night? Me, that's who. She had to get her kicks from somewhere. Yes, she got them from Saltz, but I wouldn't have hurt her because of it."

"That's hard to believe," I said. "She was cheating on you, and you'd taught Gale how to make poppets. How do we know you weren't in on it together?"

Bo's arms dropped in defeat. "Okay. The truth is that Gale wanted to make a poppet, Shelly knew about it and offered to be the guinea pig."

I shot Axel a look that said, *Likely story.*

"One night we all sat down together, and I showed Gale how to use it on Shelly. She made one of me, too." He sighed. "Shelly's dead, so she can't corroborate it. You'll just have to believe me."

"It's hard to trust any of that." Axel crossed his arms. "The dead can't confirm a story."

Bo hung his head. "I know. Ask Gale to show you the poppet of me."

I nudged Axel. "There was a male poppet with her things."

"I know." He sighed. "There was." He turned back to Bo. "Poppets are illegal."

"I know," Bo wailed. "I know they are. I'm not saying what I did was right, but I trusted Gale. Both Shelly and I did. Besides, I know I may look guilty in this, but who's had more access to magic than anyone else?"

"Who?" I had to know.

"Saltz Swift. He runs the contest. He knows where everyone is at all times. If anyone had ample opportunity not only to kill Shelly but to steal, it would've been him."

He rubbed the bags under his eyes. "Shelly had just broken their affair off. I have it on good authority that Saltz didn't take it well. So he's who you need to talk to."

"But why take the potion?" Axel slid a thumb over his jaw. "Why not just kill her? Why do it in public?"

"He was jealous," Bo exploded. Apparently he'd been keeping a few things locked up. "Shelly had taught potions before Saltz came in. He never felt that he matched up to her."

I raised a hand. "Wait. That doesn't make sense. He was the potion master before he ever even started at the school."

Bo's gaze narrowed. "That doesn't mean the man doesn't lack an inferiority complex. Why else start the affair with Shelly in the first place?"

I frowned. "Why?"

"To see if she knew something he didn't, of course. The man's horribly insecure. Can't you tell?"

No, not really. "But why would he want the potion?"

"Because he didn't think of it first!" Bo slammed a hand on the table. "Why else?" He closed his eyes and exhaled. "Look, I'm as much in the dark about this as you are. But what I do know is that I didn't do it and if anyone had reason to kill Shelly, it was Saltz. Maybe you should be targeting him instead of me."

He had a good point. If Saltz had the ego that first impressions suggested, then the fact that another teacher was smarter than him would irk Saltz to death. It wouldn't matter if he was having an affair with Shelly or not. The point would be that she was smarter than him.

I had the feeling Saltz didn't take too kindly to anyone more brilliant than himself.

Axel studied Bo for a moment longer before tugging my arm. "Let's go. I think we've learned all we're going to here."

I took the poppet and let Axel lead me from the house. Once we were secured in the Rover, I turned to him. "So you don't think he's guilty."

"Hard to tell, but I think he had a point about Saltz. Who had the most to gain by Shelly's death?"

I quirked a brow. "You think Saltz did?"

"Possibly. He would've wanted a potion like that for himself. Once he was in possession of it, he would've studied it, dissected it until he figured out the recipe. Give it a few years and everyone would forget that Shelly Seay had ever invented such a thing. He could pawn it off as his own. That's what I'd do."

I glared at him.

He chuckled. "It's what I would do if I was a criminal mastermind."

"Oh, right. There's definitely a distinction there."

"There is." He hoisted an arm over my shoulders and pulled me to him. "Glad you realize my brilliance is nothing short of criminal."

I laughed. "I'm just elated you're not really on the other side of the law."

"Same here."

We swung back by Familiar Place and picked up Betty before Axel dropped me off at the house. By the time I hit the front door I was dog-tired.

I kicked off my shoes and melted onto the couch.

"Rough day?" Cordelia stood by the kitchen door. She held a half-gallon of Witch Ice Cream, her elbow deep in the carton.

"Wow. Have you eaten all that?"

She shrugged. "It's as good a dinner as any."

I peeled off my socks and tucked my feet under me. "Since we don't have Betty to cook for us, it's slim pickings around here. I'll probably eat a bowl of marshmallows."

Cordelia snorted. "That almost sounds better than this."

I shrugged. "I doubt it." She sank onto a chair across from me and stared down at her dinner. "I really miss Betty. I never thought I'd say it. Heck, I never thought I'd admit it, but I really do."

"She'll be all right."

I hoped.

Cordelia reached over the coffee table and squeezed my knee. "You've done so much to help her. So much. We all owe you our thanks. If Amelia wasn't so wrapped up in this nonsense about being a genie, she'd be thanking you as well."

I dropped my head onto the back of the couch. "Don't thank me. I've tried and tried, but nothing has worked. It's all been a royal pain in the tush if you want the truth. The animals knew the potion. They knew every single ingredient except it still didn't work."

I raked my fingers down my face. "I give up. I've tried everything, Cordelia. I don't know what else to do."

"Of all the people I know, you're the last one to give up."

I picked through a stack of magazines on the other end of the couch in an attempt to ignore her.

"You're not talking to me."

"Because this isn't about me. It's about Betty. She was trying to save us by taking part in the potion contest."

Cordelia's jaw dropped. "What?"

I nodded. "Yep. The only way Betty would be Shelly's guinea pig was to make Shelly promise not to sell the potion to anyone. Betty was trying to save witches everywhere by her deeds. She doesn't deserve to be stuck like that."

I pointed to the toad sitting in a bowl of water in her box.

Cordelia dropped the spoon in the carton and set it aside. "You're right, she doesn't. I haven't been the best this week. I've been worried more about showing my dad how angry I am than trying to embrace him."

I tipped my head and smiled. "It's not your dad's fault he wasn't in your life."

"Oh yeah, now I know it was my mom's, so I'm ticked at her."

I laughed. "She had a very good reason. Listen, Cordelia, it wasn't her fault that your dad's power went wonky around her. She was trying to keep you safe. Both your aunts were. What if they'd wished for something and it had backfired and hurt you? Wouldn't that have been worse?"

She hung her head. "Yes. It would have been. I'm mature enough to admit that, but it still hurts. You know? It was one thing I always wanted in my life—a father. Growing up with a chaos witch for a mother wasn't easy."

"I have no doubt. But at least you have a mother and a father."

It was more than I had. I'd never known my mother, and my father had passed away without telling me about my witch lineage.

Her cheeks crimsoned. "I know. I'm sorry for being so ridiculous. That's what I mean about how you're helping Betty. You only just met this family, and you'd dive into a pit of fire to help any one of us." She rubbed her forehead. "I've been such a jerk. I'm sorry."

I shook my head. "You've had your own issues to work out. I don't think Betty would blame you for your crisis. I mean, your dad appears, tells you you're part genie but don't use your powers because they might destroy a planet—it's a lot for anyone to take in."

Cordelia laughed. "Thanks for the vote of confidence. I've been ignoring a lot of things because of it."

"Like what?"

"Garrick for one. He's been so busy with this case that it's been easy to do. He's reached out to me, but I haven't made myself emotionally available."

"Don't be so hard on yourself. Once this case is over, I'm sure Garrick would love to spend some time with the smart-mouthed Cordelia we all know and love." I unhooked my feet from under me and stretched my legs. "Want to watch some TV?"

"Sure."

I flipped on the tube, and we settled into quiet for a few minutes. It was Cordelia who broke it. "So what'd you find out tonight? Anything that will help Betty?"

"Oh, right." I'd almost forgotten, my brain was so fried. "Bo told us that he taught Gale East how to make poppets but Shelly knew all about it. And that we need to be looking into Saltz Swift if we want to know who really killed Shelly and who might have the potion."

"That's easy enough. You go to the school, break in and rummage around his office."

I laughed. "Right. So easy. But even if he did it, I doubt Saltz would keep the potion at the school. Seems he'd keep it at his house."

She shrugged. "I don't know. The school has lots of places to hide things, and his potion lab is there."

I nodded. "Oh, you're right. So it would be perfect."

"And," she added, "I happen to know on good authority that the school is hosting a fundraising dinner tomorrow night."

I sat up. "How do you know that?"

Cordelia blew on her fingers as if that proved her superior smarts. "Magic," she said mysteriously. "Kidding. Because they're all checking into the inn."

"Oh my gosh. So the school will be chock-full of folks tomorrow night?"

She smiled. "Yep. There will be so many bodies ambling around that no one will notice if a few outside witches manage to sneak in and do a little sleuthing."

A slow smile crept across my face. "Wow, Cordelia. That sounds like the best sweet-tea-witch plan ever."

Cordelia poked the air and made a square. The lines appeared with the help of her magic. "I agree. Now. Let's work out the logistics."

TWENTY-ONE

"There's going to be a huge party tonight at the school. It's the perfect way for us to get in and see if Saltz is hiding the potion anywhere."

Axel stared at me over his cup of coffee. "Aren't you forgetting something?"

My stomach knotted. What was I forgetting? "Oh, you're invited. It will be me, Cordelia and probably Amelia, but yes, I want you there as well. Obviously."

Amusement sparked in his blue eyes. I couldn't help but trace my gaze over his smooth yet sharp features—the thick razor brows, his chiseled jaw. The grace his face possessed made my heart flip-flop.

Seriously, how was he so beautiful?

"That's not what I'm talking about."

His words snapped me from my inward drool-fest. "What do you mean?"

"I was about to call Garrick and tell him what Bo said. He'll be investigating Saltz."

I scoffed. "By the time Garrick walks in, Saltz will have time to make the potion vanish or something. He's a powerful wizard, Axel, and Garrick is too nice to cast some sort of freeze spell on Saltz to stop him from doing anything. Plus, that's probably illegal."

His jaw tensed.

"You know I make sense." I leaned forward. "I'm not trying to usurp justice or anything."

He quirked a brow. "Then what are you trying to do?"

"Save Betty."

Our gazes locked until he sighed in what I hoped was defeat. The good kind of defeat, not the bad kind.

"You're forgetting something else."

I slapped a thigh. "What else could I possibly be forgetting? Saltz Swift might have the potion. Check. A whole throng of folks will be covering up the school tonight. Check. Sneak in and root through his lab. Check."

I winked at him. "Seriously, I think I've checked just about everything off the list."

"Except me."

"What do you mean?"

"Tonight's the full moon."

"Oh. I did forget." I traced a finger over my lips as I worked out the options. "Okay, well, I can come see the new building you've erected. That'll be good."

"Yes."

"And I can give you the potion I made especially for you." I smiled hopefully.

Axel sighed. "I suppose you can do that."

"Promise?" He nodded. I clapped with glee. "Yes! Finally we can see if the potion works."

I didn't want to get my hopes up. Had to keep myself in check. After all, nothing I had done so far had actually worked long term with Axel. I doubted this would, either.

But it was abso-freaking-lutely worth a heck of a shot.

"But back to reality," I said, sobering up. "I will go to the school tonight. You know that, right?"

Axel dragged his gaze from mine and sighed. "But you won't be alone?"

"No. Cordelia and Amelia will be with me. It's not like we'll be harming anyone. I'm only trying to see if Saltz has the potion. Like I said, by the time Garrick gets in there and questions him, all Saltz has to do is magically whisk the vial away. He doesn't think anyone's on to him right now. Don't you think we should keep it that way?"

"Pepper," he warned.

"Axel," I warned in return. We locked gazes and laughed. "You know I'm right. Can you trust me on this?"

He raked his fingers through his hair. "Do I have a choice?"

"Actually, no. You have no choice because I'm going in whether or not you approve. It would be nice if you did, but a gal's gotta do what a gal's gotta do."

"And you're that gal."

I winked. "You know it." I sidled up to Axel and wrapped my arms around his neck. "Besides, what's the worst that could go wrong?"

He settled his hands on my waist and pushed me gently back. "Wrong question to ask."

I rolled my eyes. "What time are you heading to the house so you can be bricked in for the night?"

"Very funny. Around four."

I kissed his nose. "See you then."

IT WAS cold that afternoon in the Cobweb Forest. Axel and I had ridden our cast-iron skillets there. He landed on a smooth turf of grass. I landed on a bed of dried leaves. Their crunch was as loud as shotgun blasts beneath my feet.

"Don't try to sneak up on anybody," I murmured.

"There's no one to sneak up on here." Axel climbed off his skillet and took my hand. "Come on."

I followed him to a hedgerow. It was the same square frame of vegetation that he'd always been chained behind. When we came around, I half expected to see his old chain linked to a concrete slab.

But that scene had vanished. The entire place was empty.

"Are you kidding?"

Axel waved a hand, and a brick structure bloomed into view.

"That is so cool. I bet you're going to tell me that magic had something to do with that."

He shook his head. "Just a touch."

"Why have you made it invisible?"

"It just makes my life easier. Keeps vandals away."

My heart sank. "You will be accepted in town."

"One day, maybe. But there are still those who don't trust me. I don't trust me either; that's why I've built this."

It was formidable. Brick and steel and windowless, no less, the structure was painted black and looked more like a charred and shriveled heart than something that would house the person I cared for one night a month.

I pressed a hand to Axel's bicep. "This will all work out."

He stiffened as he stared at the structure. "Maybe." Then he smiled down at me weakly. "You ready to chain me up? Lock me in?"

I pulled a vial from my purse. "And drug you so that you can connect with me?"

He sighed, clearly resigned to my Southern girlie powers of persuasion. "All right. But let's go inside first."

I grinned, my heart swelling in my chest. "Okay." A chilly wind sliced through the air. "It's cold out here. Do you have a heater in there?"

He barked a laugh. "No."

"Rats." I glanced around the woods. "Didn't you say earlier that the forest can take me to the school?"

He nodded. "If you ask it, it can."

"And then do I walk or fly?"

"Walk." Axel flattened his hand to the side of the brick. It shimmered before fading away.

"Cool trick."

The inside of the building was a freezer. Colder than it was outside. I hated to dose Axel and run, but that's pretty much what I was about to do.

"Too cold for you?" He said.

I shivered. "Just a touch."

He clapped his hands, and a fire roared in one corner. "Oh, thank you." I rubbed my hands in front of it and sighed. "This is miraculous."

Axel pulled off his shirt. "Do you like my digs?"

My gaze bounced around the room. Even though the outside was black, the inside was painted a much more muted color that reminded me of light lemon. He'd lined one wall with floating shelves and had a framed picture of me sitting in the center.

My lips bowed into a sort of happy pout. "You put a picture of me in here."

He wrapped his arms around me. Heat wafted off the silky-smooth skin of his chest. "Of course I have a picture of you in here." Axel nuzzled my neck. "I love you."

I patted his chest. "I love you." We stared at each other. I traced the top of his pec. "So how is this place more secure?"

Axel dropped his arms. "Once I'm in the werewolf state, no one can get in and I can't get out."

I quirked a brow. "No one?"

He sighed. "Okay, there is one way, but it's basically impossible."

"What would that be?"

"I'd have to let you in."

"As a werewolf? That is impossible."

He smirked. "You understand what I'm saying. I don't have any control as the wolf, so I can't let anyone in."

"And you can't get out."

"The walls are reinforced magically." His head snapped toward a wall. "We're losing light out there. We need to hurry."

"Let's do it." I pulled two potions from my purse and handed him one. "Since I don't know the exact dose, I figure if we just each drink one, it should be enough."

"But it won't kill me."

I elbowed his perfect abdomen. "No." Pause. "I don't think."

"Very funny." We tapped potions. "Cheers!"

"Cheers."

The potion tasted of honey as it trickled down my throat. You would think I would've tasted my own potion before now, but I honestly hadn't thought about it. I'd been more concerned with other things.

But darn, did it taste good. It didn't even need jellybeans to sweeten it. I considered that a win.

When we finished, I smiled up at Axel expectantly. His face twisted into a scowl. He doubled over.

Oh my God. I'd killed him!

I reached for Axel. "Are you okay?"

His head snapped up. Coarse dark hair sprouted from his cheeks. "Get out! You have to get out. Now!"

"Wait. I don't understand."

Axel grabbed my shoulders in a vise of death and thrust me toward the missing wall. "Go. Now!"

I twisted back as I was thrown from the building. Axel's spine bowed and protruded grotesquely. Rage and passion filled his face. His bones and muscles cracked and popped.

In that instant I knew what I'd done. I hadn't made the connection with Axel better. I hadn't helped him. I'd made it worse.

I'd brought on the wolf fast and furious. I curled my fingers in my hair trying to figure out what I'd done wrong.

"Axel!"

"Go," he roared.

"The door. The wall! You have to brick it up."

The face of the man I knew flashed before me for the briefest of seconds. My heart constricted as if a huge hand were squeezing all the life from it.

The absolute pain that flushed his features made me sick. Axel lifted one warped and distended hand. The brick reappeared, and I could no longer see what was happening inside.

I pressed my palm to the cold black brick. "Axel?"

A roar was my only response. Maybe, just maybe I could still reach him. I closed my eyes and dropped my forehead to the frigid surface. He wasn't completely the beast yet. Part of him still lived inside. I knew it did.

I entered a world of black—black walls, black floors. It was dark and didn't exist in any real time or space.

Axel?

He was only a few feet from me. I'd reached him before. I could do it again.

Axel! Can you hear me?

A shriveled voice sprouted from the darkness. I couldn't quite make it out. It just sounded low and lost, aimless.

Axel?

A roar split the dark. It pierced the air and sliced my eardrums.

"Ah!" I sprang from the wall.

He was gone. Absolutely gone. The beast had completely taken over, and it had been all my fault. What had I done wrong? Where had I messed up? Mattie and I had worked for an entire week on that potion. It should've been right. It shouldn't have caused him to become the wolf prematurely. It shouldn't have allowed the beast to consume him like this. It should have given us time together, time to tether our connection.

Breath stuttered from my lungs. I had to stay glued. I couldn't unhinge just because the potion hadn't worked. There was still so much more that needed to be done tonight.

So much more.

I inhaled a deep shot of air and pushed it out forcefully. I peered into the Cobweb Forest, squared my shoulders and said, "Okay, Forest. If you would be so kind, please lead me to the Southern School of Magic."

With that, I stepped forward, leaving Axel behind.

TWENTY-TWO

J met Cordelia and Amelia outside the school. Actually I met them in the bushes. I know. It was the most likely place to be found. I also realize that. But it worked out okay for us.

I watched as a stream of witches landed their cast-iron skillets in the circular drive. "What's happened so far?"

"Just a whole bunch of people showing up, parking their skillets." Amelia brushed a twig from my shirt. "What've you been doing? Rolling in the forest?"

"Very funny. No. I tried that potion out on Axel."

Interest sparked in her eyes. "Oh? Did it work?"

"No. Like anything and everything else I've tried with him, it didn't work." I motioned to her purse. "Did you bring Betty?"

"She's right here." Amelia patted the pouch. "Cordelia didn't want to carry her."

My cousin rolled her eyes skyward. "I didn't say I didn't want to carry her. I said you would probably be better at it, and then I said Pepper would be best because she won't drop Betty."

"Or turn her into a giant toad." The words flew from my mouth before I had a chance to stop them.

"What's that?" Cordelia frowned at me.

"It's nothing." Amelia laughed nervously. She punched me in the shoulder. "Pepper doesn't mean anything."

I rubbed the spot and nodded. "Nope. I didn't mean anything."

Cordelia's gaze dragged from one of us to the other before settling back on the scene of witches. "We need to focus. There's a whole lot of folks going inside. We should be able to sneak in soon."

"If we'd planned this right, we could've just walked in with them," I said.

Amelia nodded to the open door. "Saltz is right there greeting everyone. We won't be able to sneak in this way."

I nibbled the edge of my finger. "Then how do you suppose we can get in?"

"Let's go around back," Cordelia said. "If it's like most places, that's where the kitchen will be."

Amelia nodded. "There will be a lot of coming and going. Should be easy."

We walked the forest line to the rear of the school. There was an open door. Lots of noise and commotion floated outside.

I squeezed my cousins' hands. "It's now or never. We can do this."

We smiled to each other and proceeded to pass through the door and enter.

"Hold it right there, you three."

We froze. I shot my cousins frightened looks. They did the same to me. We slowly turned to see a squat woman wearing a white cap and smudged apron.

"Where have the three of you been?" She wagged a finger at us.

I'm sorry? None of us answered. We didn't know what to say.

The woman threw her hands up. "Never mind where you've been. You're here now. There are the trays. I want each of you to take a tray and get in there. The guests have arrived, and it's time to serve them."

She hoisted the pouch from Amelia's shoulder. "I'll store your bag in a locker. Now get in there and serve those guests before Saltz has my head."

I shot a look to my cousins. Cordelia's mouth quirked into a mischievous smile. "Well? What are we waiting for, ladies? Let's start serving."

∽

THE BEST PART ABOUT SERVING? Moving freely among the dinner guests. The worst part about serving? Avoiding Saltz Swift.

I literally had to duck or hold the hors d'oeuvres tray in front of my face while I walked.

"Well, we're in," Amelia murmured while kitchen staff piled shrimp canapés onto the silver trays.

"That we are."

Cordelia sidled up beside us. "Pepper, doesn't your stomach hurt?"

I narrowed my gaze. "No, I'm fine."

She elbowed my ribs.

"Yes, yes, it does hurt. Ow. I don't know what I ate. I have to go to the bathroom."

The cook pointed a spoon aggressively toward me. "It better not have been one of my creations. Staff doesn't eat until the rest of the party does."

"Oh, I would never dream of breaking the rules. Ow." I doubled over dramatically.

"If you start throwing up green stuff, it's your appendix." She pointed left. "Bathroom's that way. Hurry up. We ain't got all day to wait on you." She cocked an evil eye at my cousins. "You two will need to take up the slack while she's gone. Hurry. I'm almost done with the soup. They're about to sit down to dinner."

Amelia sniffed the air. "The soup smells delicious."

"You can have your bit after the others have eaten," Cook snapped. "Now get to it."

"Aye, aye, captain." Amelia saluted her with a smile.

I didn't stand around waiting to see how the Grinch would take that. I bolted from the kitchen up a side stairwell toward the staff offices. I hit the landing and stopped.

Only wall sconces that cast flickers of light across the floor lit the hallway. I held my breath and waited. No other sound filled the hallway.

I was alone. At least I hoped so. I stepped lightly toward Saltz's office and turned the knob. It would be a miracle if it was unlocked.

It was a miracle.

The door swung silently, and I crept inside. Though the office itself was little more than an elaborately decorated desk with chairs for visitors, I suspected Saltz had a personal potion room behind a door.

I mean, why wouldn't he have a personal potion room? He was the potion master.

If I had that sort of title, I would definitely own a personal potion room. It only made sense.

I crept to the door and turned the knob. As luck would have it, it opened as well. I shut it quietly behind me and flipped on a light.

Jackpot.

There were beakers and burners, jars filled with liquids and spell books everywhere.

This was exactly what I'd been looking for. I wasted no time in opening cabinets and riffling through bottles. There were so many. Dozens of vials filled with liquids that were dozens more different colors. Some were clear, others were opaque and some held potions so viscous the liquid barely moved at all when tipped.

There were so many, but none of them were the color I sought. I didn't think Saltz would tamper with the original potion. That didn't make sense. What did make sense would be to hide it in plain sight.

No one would ever suspect that he would do such a thing as to kill Shelly. After all, he wasn't even being investigated. So to keep the potion out front where anyone could see it was the most logical choice.

At least to me it was.

I sifted through bottle after bottle, rack after rack until there wasn't anyplace left to look. I didn't know how long I'd been gone, but surely the kitchen was about to serve the soup by now.

I slumped back on my heels and sighed. All of this for nothing. Axel and I had looked at everyone. We weren't any farther along in the investigation than we would have been if we'd never lifted a finger.

I exhaled a deep breath and hoisted myself to my feet. I guess there was no other choice but to let Garrick do his job.

Not that it was a bad thing. He could do his job all day long. The problem was that it meant we still didn't have any answers.

I dusted off the seat of my pants, fixed the bottles I'd moved out of place and headed to the door. I flipped off the light and quietly tiptoed through Saltz's office.

I twisted the knob and peeked. The coast was clear.

Footsteps sounded down the hall, coming from behind me. I eased the door until it was only open by a crack and peered out.

A figure cloaked in black strode into view. He moved quickly, almost like a blur. He held something in his left hand.

Light from a wall sconce struck the object. I bit my lips so I wouldn't gasp.

It was the missing potion! Shelly's. I would recognize that color anywhere. It looked like liquid sunshine. Not sure if that's what it tasted like, but that's what it looked like.

My fingers trembled. My knees quaked. Whoever it was held the potion in his hands.

But who was it?

He slipped down a stairwell. As quietly as I could, I let myself out of Saltz's office and followed. When I reached the stairwell, I realized it was the same one I'd come up. It led down to the kitchen.

I waited a moment to make sure the figure was gone before heading down. The last thing I needed was for whoever it was to hear me and know I was on to them.

I reached the kitchen and paused. Aside from my cousins and me, everyone else wore white. That was a kitchen staff essential, so I could easily mark them off the list.

I stopped and stared. The kitchen was bustling with cooks plating entrees, chopping vegetables and frying meat.

I grabbed the cook closest to the entryway. "Did you see someone come through here? He was wearing black."

The cook forearmed a line of sweat from his head. "All I can see is this meat, ma'am. I don't have time to look around."

I rushed past him but stopped the next cook. "Did you see a man run through here? He was wearing black."

The cooks repeatedly shook their heads. No one had seen him.

I reached the main cooking station where the head cook was returning from the pantry with a jar of herbs.

"Took you long enough," she said. "We're serving the soup." She pointed to a tray filled with steaming bowls. "Grab one and hand it out before it gets cold."

I grabbed her shoulders. "Did you see a man in here? A man wearing black. He would've just come through."

"I don't have time to pay attention to your dating life." She poked a stubby finger at the tray. "Now get in there and drop off those bowls."

Maybe I'd have better luck in the dining room. Perhaps in there I could figure out who I'd seen or at least be able to narrow it down.

I hoisted a tray onto my shoulder and walked toward the door, nearly smacking Amelia in the head.

"Hey," she shrieked.

"Sorry. Listen. Did you see a man walk through here? I saw someone. He had the potion. I know he did."

"No." She rubbed a spot on her forehead that I'd almost hit. "But boy are they hungry for soup so you might want to get it out there."

I entered the dining room and settled the tray down. Then I went about serving. I eyed all the guests, but none of them seemed flustered. They all sat with perfect smiles on their faces as they waited for their soup to be delivered.

Finally I saw a smiling face I recognized and trusted. Anthony stood with his back to the wall. I hooked my empty tray under my arm and practically ran over to him.

"Anthony!"

A spark of happiness flared in his eyes. "Pepper, good to see you. Looks like you're hard at work." His gaze flickered to the tray.

"Oh, that. Yeah. Listen." I pulled him to an exit door. I lowered my voice. "There's someone here who has Shelly's potion. I saw him upstairs but lost him. Have you seen anyone? Anyone at all who was carrying a vial of potion?"

The light in his eyes faded. "So you didn't recognize him." His voice sharpened. "Tell me the truth."

"No." My gaze washed down to his hand. Anthony's right fist was tight around something that looked exactly like liquid sunshine.

I gasped. "It was you."

"And you're not going to have a chance to tell anyone." Anthony grabbed me by the shirt and pulled me through a door.

TWENTY-THREE

I found myself stuck in a small, dark library. Anthony guarded the door.

I forced myself to get over my initial shock. "What? How?" But even as I asked, I knew why. I gritted my teeth. "So this is your revenge? Because you were never noticed, is that it?"

He threw back his head and laughed. The niceness in his eyes had been replaced by something so cold it sent a shiver straight to my gut.

"Yes, this is my revenge. All those years being passed over for wizards with credentials!"

Anthony dropped the vial into his pocket and steepled his pudgy fingers. "I keep this school together. I'm the person who's always called to help. I'm always needed when something goes wrong, but do I get any respect for it?"

"No?" It was a wild guess, but you know, I was pretty sure that's the answer he was looking for.

"No," he shouted. "I get no respect. So now they're going to know who runs things. They all will. Once they eat their soup."

"The soup?"

He shot me a smug smile.

A stone dropped in my stomach. *The soup.* When no one had been looking, Anthony dosed the soup with potion.

"You mean to turn all of them to toads."

All of them. Out there. Turned to frogs. I couldn't allow that to happen. No way. I shoved him to the side and headed toward the door. I'd just brushed my fingers against the knob when I stopped.

I literally couldn't move.

"Oh, Pepper Dunn. So smart, but not smart at all."

Against my will, my legs danced around until I was facing Anthony once again.

"Your grandmother should've taught you that you never let another witch or wizard take things from you—like your hair, your blood."

My skin prickled from a chill that wasn't created by ordinary means. Anthony held a poppet in his hands. A poppet that I'd practically handed him when he'd snatched a hair from my coat the night I attended the witch support group, and the blood he'd gathered the day I'd scratched myself on the front door of the school.

Anthony was right. I'd willingly given him power over me. I'd practically handed myself to him on a silver platter.

He'd used my blood and hair to create a poppet that perfectly resembled me.

I pushed aside the fear that rose in my belly and stared him down. "What are you going to do?"

"I'm going to make sure you don't interfere." Anthony turned the poppet and stared at the doll's face. "There are so many ways I can do that. I can simply leave you in here while they all turn to toads. But that's not really good enough, is it? You'll want to help them, won't you? You'll do everything you can to get in there and save those people."

"I would've saved Shelly if I could have."

He threw back his head and laughed. "Shelly was so stupid. She told me her plan but wouldn't share the potion's recipe. I knew as soon as she revealed what her potion was that I had to have it. You see, Pepper. That's the thing about being me—no one ever thought I could do something like kill Shelly. She certainly didn't. Why would she? How could sweet little Anthony, whipping boy to the world, have it in him to kill someone?"

A bitter laugh escaped his lips. "But I fooled her. I knew Shelly and her boyfriend had worked with Gale East on poppets. Gale told me herself. So I did my own research, found out how to do it and made sure Gale was at the potion competition. None of that was hard. Not at all."

"And no one would ever think it was you."

"Brilliant, isn't it?" Anthony wagged the poppet at me. "And now all I have to do is get rid of you. Make sure you don't interfere. Ever. With any of it ever again."

Anthony rubbed his chin like any good cartoon villain. "But what to do with you? Turn your head until your blood vessels pop? Break all your bones?" He scoffed. "Too agonizing. And probably you'll scream too much. Perhaps I'll just smash your head with a candlestick."

He laughed maniacally. "Mr. Anthony did it in the library with a candlestick. How wonderful!"

He lifted a candlestick from a side table. My heart thundered against my rib cage. I wanted him gone, away, but my magic didn't work. I was under the spell of a poppet. The only thing I could think of was Axel.

I'd never be able to say goodbye. I wished he was here just so I could see him one last time.

Oh, and my family. And I never helped Betty and now the entire Southern School of Magic would be knee-deep in toads. Not only would it be very empty and amphibious, but it would also be creepy.

Yes, I know, strange thoughts entered my mind at the weirdest of times, but when you're staring death in the face, you don't have much control over what goes through your head.

Anthony lifted the candlestick just as the door opened.

"Oh! Pepper, what're you doing?"

It was Amelia. My back was to her so I couldn't see her, but I had one shot.

160

"I wish that poppet stayed in Anthony's hands." It was a long shot, counting on the fact that her father hadn't locked her genie talents up yet.

"Pepper, no," Amelia shouted.

The poppet whisked from Anthony. I felt a huge release as I tipped forward.

"No!" Anthony grasped air to catch it.

But he couldn't catch where it was going—straight into Amelia's hands.

"Amelia, get out of here!"

Right as Amelia turned to run, the strangest thing happened. She suddenly shrank with a pop and a crunch, and ended up on the ground.

Amelia had turned into a toad. My poppet fell to the floor beside her.

Amelia hopped off into a dark corner. Probably for the best. This room was no place for a toad. Not with Anthony on the loose.

I careened across the floor to snatch it up. As my fingers curled to grab the wax imitation of me—red hair, big brown eyes, a slash of bangs—it lifted from the floor and zipped across the room.

I planted my palms on the wood and hoisted myself up. I didn't have to look around to know what had happened.

Anthony had control of the poppet. The entire school had been turned into toads. I didn't even have to open the door to know that. Great. It was up to me to stop Anthony because everyone else was literally a toad.

"You worked so hard, Pepper. So very hard to foil me. But you can't. I've thought this through too hard and too long to be ruined now. Everything I've done has been to reach this moment. The one point where I will win."

"And what do you win?" I turned and glared at him. "There's no one around to congratulate you. To tell you what a great job you've done. No one has watched you succeed. No one. You've turned them all to toads, but you don't even know which one is Saltz."

I pointed to the door. "If you went out there right now, you'd see a mess of toads that made the place look more like a bad seventies disaster movie than your victory. You don't know one toad from another. All you know is that you've won. But what have you won if there's no one to witness it?"

Anthony's gaze fell to the floor. "I know. That's enough."

I hitched a shoulder. "But what? The knowledge that you stole a potion by killing a witch and then using that potion to create a sea of toads? Doesn't sound like much of a victory if you ask me."

His face crimsoned. Anthony's eyes bugged, and his nostrils flared. "I've won, okay. If I say I've won, I have."

"Sure. You've won. You made a poppet out of me. Got for it. Destroy me with a candlestick. You've beaten us all."

Okay, so my plan at this point was to make Anthony angry enough that he either dropped my poppet or his focus. So far neither had worked.

I had one more shot. I thought him away, gone. I wanted him back.

My legs sprinted forward. I had to fight to keep myself from running into Anthony.

"Your power doesn't work when I have the poppet." He shook his head. "Poor new witch." He caressed the poppet's head. A shiver ran down my spine. It was like watching myself be violated by this pudgy man with curly hair. Ew.

Anthony continued. "It's hard to be bested. But don't worry, I'm about to put you out of your misery."

Stall him. I had to stall and think. "Anthony!"

He bounced the candlestick in his palm. "Yes?"

"What happens now? You've bested me. You've reduced the school staff to toads. What's it all for?"

He threw his head back and released an air-splitting cackle. "What happens next is when the students return, I'll be running this school. Pepper Dunn will have potioned the entire staff. Luckily I caught you, but not before you threw yourself out of a window. Oh, and the potion will be all used up, so if we want to save Saltz, we'll have to perform blood magic. No one will want to do that, of course, so the school will now be mine to run."

He grinned wickedly. "After all, I'm the only person who knows how to make things work here anymore. Everyone will be a toad!"

"You think it'll be that easy? You think they'll all accept what you've done?"

Before I asked it, I knew it was a stupid question. Dang it.

"Oh, I'll be accepted all right. What choice do they have? I'll replace Saltz as head of the school. It will be wonderful. It will all be truly wonderful."

He raised his hands like he was in a hallelujah choir. "Finally, I'll receive the credit I deserve." Anthony slowly lowered his arms and pinpointed his focus on me. "Now all I have to do is get rid of you."

He raised the candlestick. I was paralyzed. Unable to move. I closed my eyes because this was it. It was over. *I* was over. My life was gone.

Hey, at least I'd done some good before I'd been called up to heaven.

A loud crash sent me sprawling across the floor. I opened my eyes. A window had shattered. Glass shards littered the wooden floor.

I blinked, unsure of exactly what I was seeing.

A huge mass of fur and fangs stood in the room. The beast shook its coat, sending more glass flying.

"Oh my Lord," I whispered.

The werewolf snarled and snapped. Its tail lashed; its fangs gnashed. Saliva dripped from its mouth.

"Axel?" How could it be? How could he be standing here when he was supposed to be locked inside an impenetrable box?

Are you okay? His voice filled my head. In that instant I realized what had happened.

It had worked! The potion had worked. But there was no time to rejoice. Anthony still clutched my poppet. He still had control of me.

Yes, I'm fine. Axel, he has—

I see it. I'm on it.

The werewolf padded toward Anthony. I did a quick check to make sure I wasn't covered in glass and rose.

"Stay back," Anthony said. "What do you want? Don't hurt me! I'm mostly blubber. You won't like how I taste."

I did think the blubber part was true and not because of his physical appearance. Anthony had lied about who he was. He wasn't a good guy at all. He was a bad, bad person.

The wolf released a hair-raising growl.

I extended my palm. "If I were you, I'd hand over the poppet."

Anthony clutched it to his chest. "Never!"

I fisted a hand to my hip. "Okay, then." I patted the Axel's flank and said in my biggest puppy-dog voice, "You ready to eat some meat?"

"Okay, okay. It's yours." Anthony thrust out his arm.

I took the wax figure and held it to my chest. I glanced at the wolf. "Do whatever you want to him."

"No!" Anthony cowered onto his knees. "No! I'm sorry! I'll fix it. I'll give up the potion so you can change everyone!"

He handed me the mostly empty vial.

"Let's hope this is enough to fix things. Keep an eye on him while I call the police."

I left Axel snarling and snapping at Anthony to fetch my phone and call Garrick. I entered a dining room full of hopping toads. I picked over their fat bodies and made it the kitchen, where I retrieved my phone.

Garrick answered on the first ring. I inhaled a deep shot of air.

"I'm at the Southern School of Magic. You'd better get over here quick. We've got a situation."

TWENTY-FOUR

*G*arrick arrived not long after with a squad of men. With their help we fed a teaspoonful of soup to all the toads, effectively returning them to normal.

Needless to say folks were a little startled that a giant werewolf was curled up by the hearth in one of the great rooms, but hey, that werewolf had managed to save their skins, so to speak, so no one had a bad word to say.

"You've done a great job, Pepper."

Garrick placed a hand on my shoulder. I'd just finished dosing the last toad.

"Thanks, Garrick. I know you didn't want us to get involved."

"But if *we* hadn't, we never would've saved the entire school from a life of toad-dom." Cordelia wrapped an arm around Garrick's waist. She shot him a bright smile full of sunshine. "Now would we have?"

He tipped his head down. His dark eyes were full of love. "No, we wouldn't have." He glanced back at me. "Y'all have done a great job."

"I would say so." Saltz Swift approached. "I suppose I owe a huge thank-you to you and your cousins, Pepper."

"And to the werewolf." I nodded to Axel.

Saltz's lower lip stiffened briefly. "Thank you, wolf." He turned to Garrick. "I suppose Anthony will be dealt with accordingly?"

"He will. He's already admitted to killing Shelly and to using the potion on all of y'all."

"Good." Saltz turned to me. "And Miss Dunn, will you be taking me up on my offer to teach a few lectures on familiars? We could use your talents here."

I glanced around at my cousins and to Axel. He didn't say anything, but I could tell he thought it was a good idea.

"I'd love to," I said.

"Good. I will contact you with details. Now I must ensure our patrons are safe after their ordeal." With that, he turned in a grand sweeping gesture and walked away.

Amelia bounded up. "Wow. That was so crazy. And wow! Axel! He's sitting there as if he doesn't care about us."

I smiled. "He doesn't. Well, not enough to eat us, anyway."

Amelia smiled. "So what did it?"

"It was the potion I created for the competition. At first I didn't think it had worked, but apparently after I left Axel tonight, it did. At one point Anthony had me cornered. I reached out to Axel, and a little while later he appeared."

I glanced at the wolf. "How'd you get out of the building?"

With my powers. I have complete control and could work the magic needed.

Impressive. "He used his magic. I don't know if the connection will work next time, but it was awesome that it did tonight." I cocked my head. "And Amelia, thanks for having broken genie powers."

Cordelia's jaw dropped. "I thought your dad was supposed to suspend your abilities."

She cringed. "Well, I asked him to wait just a couple of days. So he did." She shook her head briskly. "But don't worry; first thing tomorrow morning I'm getting them locked down."

I cocked my chin. "They did us a favor tonight. Saved my life until Axel could show up." I shot her a wide smile. "Thanks for keeping me alive."

"Who's keeping who alive?"

That voice made my heart swell. I opened my arms wide. "Betty!"

My grandmother waddled to us. Her corncob pipe was shoved in her mouth, and she wore a velour jumpsuit with racing stripes blazing down the sides.

I wrapped her in a hug. "We're so glad to have you back!"

She tugged her curls. "I'm glad to be back. I thought I'd never get out of that toad's body. It's one thing to eat crickets for one meal, but every single one? Disgusting. I need some variety in my diet."

I threw my head back with laughter. My cousins did the same. It was good to have my family back. It was awesome, actually.

Betty pointed to Axel. "I like him that way, lounging on the floor. Think it'll last?"

I shrugged. "Not sure. But I can't wait to find out."

TWENTY-FIVE

*S*o even Magnolia Cove's staunchest werewolf haters had to admit that Axel Reign had saved the day—literally. If it hadn't been for him, there was no doubt I would've ended up dead and the school would've been run by Anthony, a deranged psycho.

Maybe using deranged to describe psycho is redundant. Either way, he was a psycho who ended up behind bars.

Thank goodness.

As for Amelia, her dad did arrest her genie powers. Frankly they needed to be arrested, but not before she managed one last wish—and did so successfully.

I stood in the living room, arms flared and hope ballooning in my chest.

"You can do it." Bean gave Amelia an encouraging grin. "Pepper, keep your thoughts focused and pure."

"Are you ready?" I said to Amelia.

She nodded. "As ready as an Easter egg."

I quirked a brow.

"I just made it up." Amelia shrugged. "But I am. Go on, now, cuz."

I closed my eyes. "I wish for my hair to return to its original color."

Amelia's back bowed as if the wish had hit in her the solar plexus.

The air shimmered and bent. My cousin puffed up her chest, and a current of magic streamed through the air and sprinkled over my head.

I held my breath until my scalp finished tingling. I peeked open one eye. "Well?"

Bean clapped Amelia on the shoulder. "Take a look."

I peered into the mirror in the living room. A wide smile split my face. "Oh my gosh, Amelia. It looks perfect!"

It did. My honey and crimson hair had returned. It hung in loose beautiful waves down my back. I plumped the ends before crossing to Amelia and wrapping her in a gigantic hug.

"You did great."

"Thank you, but I'm still going on hiatus from my powers. At least until I learn how to really grant wishes. If I even can."

A thought struck me. "Bean, if you can stop Cordelia and Amelia from using their powers, why weren't you able to do that with your own? You know, when you and Morgan were married to Mint and Licky."

Bean stroked his chin. "That's a good question, Pepper. Morgan and I both tried. We wanted nothing more than to shut our powers off, but I think we have too much genie blood running through our veins. There's no way to know if our daughters will be able to control their talents, but we hope so. Wish granting takes skill and focus. There's a lot that goes into it."

Amelia beamed. "I'm getting better, but there's still a lot more to learn."

Amelia gave her father a huge hug, and I thanked them both for their help.

Cordelia had decided to forgive her father as well and was beginning to spend more time with Morgan, which made me happy. I wanted my cousins to be happy. I was happy. They should be happy.

Hugo and I left for Familiar Place. It was a cold day, but believe it or not Betty had knitted Hugo a dragon sweater. Yeah, I know. Totally crazy but dragons are cold-blooded and they survive best when warm.

So Betty made him a sweater.

Y'all, it surprised even me.

We'd only been in the store a few minutes when the door swung open and in strode Axel.

"To what do I owe the pleasure of this visit?"

He raked his fingers through his ebony hair and grinned. "Do I need a reason or can I just visit you?"

"Oh?" I quirked a brow. "Is this a 'just 'cause' visit?"

He hooked his fingers in my jeans and tugged me into a hug. Most girls might not want a big alpha werewolf to do something like that, but I loved it.

I curled my fingers into his concrete biceps right before his lips claimed mine. His mouth was hot and sweet, and he tasted of cinnamon.

"Been eating jellybeans?" I said when we parted for air.

"How'd you know? I've got an entire jar of them at the house."

"I could help you finish them off."

He hitched a brow. "Is that a promise?"

I laughed and threw my arms around his neck. "I'm so glad. Out of everything that's happened, all the trials and tribulations, I'm so happy that we made it. We succeeded." I sighed. "How did it feel?"

He threaded his fingers through mine and rocked back. "To be in control when I'm the wolf?"

I nodded.

"Amazing. Best feeling ever."

He sat in a chair. I knelt down and pressed my forehead to his. "We make a great team."

"That we do." He tugged me into his lap.

It felt so good to be held by Axel. So right. My heart was full of love, absolutely filled to brimming.

I took his hand and studied it. Long, lean fingers, thick sinewy muscles ran through. It was perfect. He was perfect. We were perfect.

"I'm thinking," I said.

"Yes? You can say anything. Whatever you want. There's nothing to hide from me. Ever."

I pressed my lips together. Axel gently tipped my face until we locked gazes. "What?"

"Well, I was thinking that maybe, just maybe I'm ready for the next step in our relationship."

His eyelids flared. "Are you?"

"Maybe."

"No need to rush it. And no need to do a maybe on it. You be sure, 'cause when you are, I'll be here."

"But I think maybe I am."

Axel chuckled. He lifted me like I weighed nothing more than cotton and slid out from under me. He rose and wrapped his arms around my waist.

"So tiny," he murmured. "But I want you to be ready. No maybes. Talk to me when you are. I'm not going anywhere."

"But…"

He jerked his head stiffly. "No maybes." His eyes clouded as if there was something more Axel wasn't telling me. Something important. "You mean too much for anything to be a maybe."

He kissed the back of my hand. "We on for dinner tonight?"

I winked. "We sure are. Oh," I said as he started to leave, "what happened with that puzzle box?"

He smiled. "Empty. When I finally got it open, there wasn't one thing in it."

I shrugged. "Probably for the best."

Axel gave me another kiss and left. I sucked on my teeth. "Something's up with him. Don't you think so, Hugo? The way he shot me down?"

The dragon looked up from the bone he was gnawing. He didn't answer, but I didn't expect one.

I'd just settled down when the door blew open again. This time Betty entered. Her face was beet red and she was huffing, hard.

"Pepper, I've got news for you. Bad news."

I froze, unsure if I should be more terrified of the news or of how dramatic Betty was being.

"What is it?"

"I told them not to, but they did. The council cast a secret vote today, Pepper. A vote that's going to change this town."

"Should I sit?"

She pushed me into a chair.

"I guess I'll sit." I frowned. "It can't be that bad."

"It is. It is that bad." She paced the room like she was about to start spewing battle plan instructions.

"What happened?"

She sucked in a deep breath. "The council just approved Rufus Mayes to reenter Magnolia Cove."

I spoke slowly as I tried to wrap my head around the news. "Why? So he can visit?"

She pressed her palms into the counter and leaned over, locking gazes with me. "No, not so he can visit. So he can live here. Forever."

I gulped. Holy crap. This was news and not necessarily the good kind. "Well, I guess Magnolia Cove's about to get a thousand times more interesting."

Betty nodded. "You can count on it."

ALSO BY AMY BOYLES

SWEET TEA WITCH MYSTERIES

SOUTHERN MAGIC

SOUTHERN SPELLS

SOUTHERN MYTHS

SOUTHERN SORCERY

SOUTHERN CURSES

SOUTHERN KARMA

SOUTHERN MAGIC THANKSGIVING

SOUTHERN MAGIC CHRISTMAS

SOUTHERN POTIONS

SOUTHERN FORTUNES

SOUTHERN GHOST WRANGLER MYSTERIES

SOUL FOOD SPIRITS

HONEYSUCKLE HAUNTING

BLESS YOUR WITCH SERIES

SCARED WITCHLESS

KISS MY WITCH

QUEEN WITCH

QUIT YOUR WITCHIN'

FOR WITCH'S SAKE

DON'T GIVE A WITCH

WITCH MY GRITS

FRIED GREEN WITCH

SOUTHERN WITCHING

Y'ALL WITCHES

HOLD YOUR WITCHES

SOUTHERN SINGLE MOM PARANORMAL MYSTERIES

The Witch's Handbook to Hunting Vampires

The Witch's Handbook to Catching Werewolves

The Witch's Handbook to Trapping Demons

ABOUT THE AUTHOR

Amy Boyles grew up reading Judy Blume and Christopher Pike. Somehow, the combination of coming of age books and teenage murder mysteries made her want to be a writer. After graduating college at DePauw University, she spent some time living in Chicago, Louisville, and New York before settling back in the South. Now, she spends her time chasing two preschoolers while trying to stir up trouble in Silver Springs, Alabama, the fictional town where Dylan Apel and her sisters are trying to master witchcraft, tame their crazy relatives, and juggle their love lives. She loves to hear from readers! You can email her at amy@amyboylesauthor.com.

Printed in Great Britain
by Amazon

15820381R00103